ATTACK OF THE 3-D ZOMBIES

JOHN CADY

LITTLE GREMLINS
D & T

This book is dedicated to my amazing wife and my wonderful children.

1

_____

WHEN YOU'RE A KID – long before you know any better – there are
two kinds of rules. You have the ones only a fool wouldn't follow, and
you have the ones that are – by your logic – made to be broken. Well,
there was this one October when my buddy Will and I found out the
hard way just how easy it could be to confuse the two.

Zombies: Too Close for Comfort had just hit theaters a week earlier,
and pretty much everyone and his mother had already seen it opening
weekend; well, maybe not their mothers since they typically didn't
like stuff like zombies, but you get the idea. It was in 3-D, too, which
made it even more desirable. There was no way we were going to miss
out on this experience. We even went as zombies like it was already
Halloween, even though that was still a couple of weeks away. Before
you poke fun at us for it, you should know that a lot of other people
did the same opening night. We certainly weren't the only super fans.
Nothing was going to stop us; that was until we heard the unthink-
able. If you can believe it, they were actually checking I.D.'s at the
ticket counter. As expected, it was rated R. And it was the real kind of
rated R – the kind they didn't take any chances with. There was
violence, curse words, and probably a bunch of other stuff we weren't
supposed to see, like kissing on the lips. Now that I think of it, I guess

it made all of the sense in the world that they were making sure people were old enough to see it. I mean, if anything was bound to bring on nightmares, this was probably it.

"Oh well," I said with a sigh, "so much for that. What else do you want to see?"

"*What?*" Will asked, incredulously. "You mean to tell me you're gonna give up just like that? Since when are you, John Sullivan, a quitter? Aren't you the kid who still wanted to play Capture the Flag at camp with a sprained ankle?"

That was a dirty trick. Sure, bring up the time when I was at my bravest to get me to do something I could get into a lot of trouble for. What ten-year-old boy could back down from any sort of challenge after hearing that? Why did he have to pull my man card years before we even knew there was such a thing?

I couldn't help but notice we were the only ones in line dressed like zombies. I don't think I could have felt more foolish. It definitely felt like everyone was staring at us, even if they weren't.

"We're the only ones dressed up," I whispered.

Will's eyes quickly widened. I think he thought I was blaming him. Granted, it was his idea to dress up. However, I was on board fairly quickly. It took zero arm-twisting to hook me in.

"I didn't know," he replied. "I mean, you saw them on the news last week just like I did."

He was right, but it did kind of feel like we were going trick-or-treating a week or even the day after Halloween. Okay. Maybe it didn't feel *that* awkward, but you get the gist of it. I'm telling you, if even one other person was dressed up then I would have felt much better. I kept checking the door and hoping, but it was all for naught. No one else showed up in costume. I would say we were the only ones who looked the part, but, then again, we weren't actually in the movie. We just desperately wanted to watch it.

"Here goes nothing," Will said when it was our turn to pay.

In hindsight, I wish he was right. I seriously wish nothing had happened. I will say this, though, the look on the guy's face did lead me to believe nothing was going to happen.

"Hmm. Let me guess," he began, with a smirk. "You boys are here to see *Zombies?*"

We nodded in unison. *Boy!* It still had this bizarre trick-or-treating feel to it. In fact, my hands were even itching to hold a pillow case open, if you can believe it.

"In 3-D?" he continued, just as snotty as before. I could tell he wasn't the nicest guy in the world.

Again, we nodded. His eyes widened as though he couldn't wait to hand us our tickets and glasses.

"So, which one of you drove here?" he asked.

Um, what? We flashed each other the same confused look we did the year before when my parents said we could stay up to watch the ball drop on New Year's Eve. Needless to say, they knew we wouldn't make it.

"Neither one of us," I answered. "My mom dropped us off."

"Oh," he said, pretending to be surprised. You can sort of tell when somebody's faking it. "Huh. So, then, how old *are* you boys? Nine? Ten? El…"

"Ten," we answered. I didn't really want to show our cards just yet, but it was pretty obvious we weren't old enough to drive. All of the zombie make-up in the world couldn't hide the fact that we weren't quite teenagers yet. And, besides, neither one of us was particularly tall for our age. We looked every bit like fifth graders.

"Aw, man," he began, with a frown that clearly wasn't all the way genuine. "Sorry, boys, but you need to be seventeen to see this one. We wouldn't want you to have any nightmares. Right?"

We were both just about ready to throw in the towel. We had given it a shot, and we unfortunately ran head-on into a ticket booth operator who was a stickler for rules. I don't think he even took into consideration the fact that we had gone to the trouble of turning ourselves into zombies – for the movie's second weekend no less. If anyone deserved to have the rules bent just this once in their favor, it was us.

"Well, this stinks," said Will, dejectedly. "Come on. I'll call my mom."

I hoped she wasn't out running errands or something. Or, if she was, then I hoped her errands were at least in the mall attached to the theater. After all, she wasn't planning on picking us up for another two hours or so. That was the deal. *My* mom dropped us off, and *his* mom was supposed to pick us up.

We began our slow walk of shame back to the lobby when Will noticed something that might interest us on a poster for one of the other movies.

"Hey!" he shouted. "*Dog On It is also in 3-D!*"

At first, I thought he'd gone off the deep end. I had no urge to waste my allowance on a movie about a talking dog competing in the X Games, and I figured Will felt the same way. Come to think of it, though, it does sound like it would have made for a pretty cool 3-D movie. Still, there weren't likely to be any zombies in it, and we did have a fixing for zombies.

"So what?" I asked. "I don't want to see that. It's for little kids."

Will shook his head as though *I* was the one who had lost his mind.

"You really don't see what I'm getting at here?" he asked. "Seriously?"

I shook my head.

"Take a look at the start time," he suggested.

I glanced up at the screen above the ticket booth. All I noticed was it was starting in a matter of minutes.

"So?" I asked. "Do you want to go to it or not?"

Once again, he shook his head.

"No," he said. "But I do want to buy a ticket for it."

My confused expression must have given him all of the reason he needed to walk me through the rest of his plan.

"We buy tickets to *Dog On It*, we grab our 3-D glasses, and we sneak into *Zombies: Too Close for Comfort.*"

I wish I could tell you I told him it was a bad idea and that we shouldn't do something that dishonest, but truth be told I thought it was a brilliant plan. He was a genius in my book. It seemed foolproof. At the time, I couldn't poke one hole in it. Granted, I *was* too excited to even try.

"I'm in," I said, and immediately shook his hand. It was by no means a deal with the devil, but he did sort of have a devilish grin going. In fact, I'm sure we both did. Oddly enough, ours probably paled in comparison to the ticket booth operator's when he handed us our 3-D glasses for *Dog On It*.

_____

2

WE WALKED RIGHT past *Dog On It* and straight into *Zombies: Too Close for Comfort*. It was already pretty dark in there, aside from a flashlight-happy usher who was patrolling the stairs on the opposite side of the theater. It wasn't so dark in there that he couldn't make us out, but he blinded us with his light anyways. None of the people sitting in the row between us seemed all too pleased with him, which was a good thing since we might have needed them on our side once he realized we weren't allowed in there.

"Hey! You two!" he shouted, right before he was shushed by just about everyone there. This didn't seem to faze him any though.

"Who are you here with?" he continued, side-stepping a collection of knees.

"Be quiet, buddy," someone from the row said.

I couldn't make out exactly who had said it because they were all staring at the screen, but I suppose it didn't matter.

"I will once I get those kids out of here," he replied.

"Who?" the guy closest to me asked. "These kids?"

He suddenly reached up and grabbed hold of my shirt. After the shock wore off, I tried to tear myself free. It didn't take too long. I could probably chalk it up to a case of buttery fingers brought upon from repeatedly digging into his box of popcorn.

"*Quick! Move!*" I shouted, before practically knocking Will to the floor on my way up the stairs to another row – preferably one with two empty seats.

"*Will!*" I whispered, once I found a couple. "Get up here."

He scurried into the seat beside mine. Meanwhile, the dude with the flashlight was causing a ruckus a few rows down. We saw his flashlight land on the floor and roll away; we could only assume the rest of him had landed there, too.

"You know what?" we heard him shout. "This isn't even worth it. Congrats, you brats! I hope you have nightmares tonight!"

"Be quiet," somebody said, from *our* row of all places.

Not too long into the movie and before any of the zombies had the chance to get up close and personal with us, Will's stomach started to growl.

"I'm wicked hungry," he moaned. He sounded a little whiney, but I didn't call him on it. I didn't want to embarrass him in front of all of the older kids. Plus, I was kind of hungry myself.

"I know," I said. "Me, too. But we can't go out to the snack bar. If they catch us, they'll kick us out before we even see one zombie."

Before I could say anything else, we were covered in popcorn from the first real scare the movie had to offer. That is to say the woman sitting directly in front of us tossed like half of her bucket over her shoulder and into Will's lap when a zombie walked off the screen and into her row. Let's just say the effects were pretty impressive and the 3-D work was top shelf.

"I guess we don't have to go to the snack bar now," I joked.

"I'm just glad she didn't have her soda in her hand," Will whispered.

Very true. I mean, it was bad enough getting all of that butter on us. Add a soda shower to the mix and Mom wouldn't have been too pleased.

Even though it was an added bonus, the little popcorn we shared between us didn't do much in the way of filling our bellies. My stomach was on the verge of growling.

I found myself staring at the door, going over the odds of us being caught in my mind. Suddenly, the sound of screams and the vision of popcorn flying through the air caused me to snap out of it. This gave me an idea.

"I think I know how to get us more popcorn," I explained. "Come on."

I slowly stood up, scanning the theater for our flashlight-wielding friend. I didn't see him anywhere, so I made my move. Row by row, we made our way down to floor level. Anywhere we found two seats or more together, we took a seat. I'd be lying if I said we got showered in popcorn every time, but we did luck out at least twice; and, in one instance, we even got hit with some Sno-Caps. Will could take them or leave them, but I'd always been a fan. My aunt used to keep a jar of them in her kitchen. I raided that thing every chance I got.

By the time the movie ended, we weren't hungry anymore. We missed a lot of the action, but we saw enough. The title said it all. Those zombies got way too close, and it's nearly impossible to make yourself comfortable when you're on the edge of your seat.

Once the credits began to roll, I stood up and made for the door. I was still wearing the glasses.

"Hey, hold on," Will nervously blurted out, grabbing hold of my shoulder.

"The movie's over," I said. "Who cares if they kick us out now?"

As we approached the 3-D glasses receptacle, I went to casually remove my glasses to toss them in, but it turned out to be anything but casual. They wouldn't budge. I didn't know what was going on. I couldn't even say they were tangled up in my hair because it wasn't nearly long enough for that to be the case. It literally felt like they were glued to my head.

I turned to Will to see what he could make of this turn of events and maybe even enlist his help with them, but, if you can believe it, he had the exact same problem. *This was crazy.* Audience member after audience member slid past us, dropping their glasses in. For the most part, they completely ignored us. Some of them, however, looked a little annoyed that we were holding up traffic. Little did they know, we had an emergency on our hands – or rather on our head.

"What the heck is going on here?" Will finally asked.

He wasn't panicky yet. He mostly just looked confused. Who could blame him? I felt the same way.

The panic didn't set in until we stepped out into the lobby to find some help.

3

THE PLACE WAS PACKED – way more crowded than when we came in. Actually, it was more crowded than I'd ever seen it, and I'd been there for a few opening nights. They were nothing like this, and a couple of them were hugely anticipated movies that ended up making a killing at the box office. And, if you can believe it, a good number of them were dressed like zombies. Unbelievable. I wondered where they were a couple of hours earlier when Will and I were busy looking foolish. I rolled my eyes, though nobody could tell – what with the glasses still on.

I started scanning the lobby for somebody who worked there. Honestly, I would have even settled for that jerk at the ticket booth. He was nowhere to be found though. There was nobody manning the booth, which was crazy considering the amount of people waiting to get into the next showing of *Zombies: Too Close for Comfort*. The place was mobbed. His boss was probably going to be pretty upset with him.

I thought for sure he was in for it once I saw all of the costumed fans headed our way. They didn't seem too eager to wait around for him to let them in. The next show didn't start for another half-hour or so. I figured they were just making sure they got a good seat.

At one point, one of them had his eyes locked on me. It must have been because of my costume, I thought. I expected him to ask me how it was. The closer he got though, the less it looked like a costume. He looked way too real for me. I'll admit it. I was a little scared. Realistic costumes always used to get to me. I don't know what it was about them. The less of the person I could see, the more it worried me. Weird, right?

I think this guy would have scared just about anyone though. I mean, to be fair, he not only had the look and the walk down pat, but he also had the right sound. People hardly ever get that right. A lot of them, myself included, sound cheesy when they try it out. Not this guy though. He could have won an award for crying out loud. He was that good.

I got ready to give him my review, which was going to be a quick one, but he caught me by surprise when he reached for me. His right hand was just about to my shoulder when I finally backed away from him. He just missed me with his swipe.

Quick as anything, I looked to Will for some sort of a response, but he too had something strange to contend with. He was literally shaking in his boots – well, his sneakers. He started to back away from *something*, but there was nothing there from what I could see.

"*Will?*" I shouted.

He snapped out of it and quickly glanced over at me.

"Um, we need to leave," he nervously muttered. "I'm scared. This isn't fun anymore."

I can't say I was expecting that. After all, we had just sat through one of the scariest movies of all time according to one reviewer, and I didn't cover my eyes at all – not once. Before I could get this point across to him, however, another guy in a zombie getup tried to grab me.

"You're right," I agreed, glancing around nervously. More and more of them were coming our way. They were coming out of the woodwork. I'm still not sure what that means, but my grandfather used to say it all of the time. I got the feeling they weren't trying to find their seat before everyone else. Nope. I got the feeling they were trying to get at us. "We really need to get out of here."

I tried once again to get my glasses off, but, just like before, they wouldn't budge.

"Try yours, again," I requested.

He tried tugging on his, but all it resulted in was his head jerking forward. He shook his hands in desperation as if he had something stuck to them.

"Why is this happening?" he asked.

Suddenly, he looked as though a thought had crept into his head that should have been there all along. He instantly perked up. Then, without any kind of a warning, he reached over and gave my arm a terrific pinch. As if I didn't have enough on my plate, now I was getting pinched.

"*Ouch!*" I shouted, rubbing the spot where he got me. "This isn't a dream!"

We took the long way around the snack bar on our way to the exit. I'll admit it, I just didn't want to make my way through all of the crazies who were there for the next show. If they were anything like the ones who went overboard in grabbing at us, then I wanted *nothing* to do with them. It's normal for us kids to goof around like that. When grown-ups do it though, it's just plain weird – maybe even scary.

"What the..." Will started to say as we rounded the snack bar.

He was motioning to the dining area we were planning on cutting through. There they were again, headed our way. They were taking the long way to the theater.

"Why are they messing with us like this?" he continued. "They're not gonna be able to find a good seat."

"I don't think they care," I answered, a little confused myself.

"So, what's the plan then?" he asked. "Do we make a mad dash for the exit or do we calmly walk there and hope they'll leave us alone?"

I looked closely to see if any of them were getting a kick out of giving us the willies, but none of them seemed willing to break character. None of them so much as cracked a smile. They were good. That's for sure.

"Let's just walk to the exit," I said. "We don't want any of the kids from school to see us freaking out. If they do, we'll never hear the end of it."

"You're right," Will agreed. "Kids will be trying to scare us every chance they get."

A week or so earlier, a fourth grader ran screaming like a little girl from a bee, and he hadn't even been stung. From then on, the kids at school buzzed at him left and right. All I could picture in the meantime was a horde of students doing a zombie walk down the hallway every time they saw one of us.

As we walked, a bunch of them sort of formed a wall in front of us. They were waiting for us. No doubt about it. I felt like a wuss doing it, but I glanced back over to the other side of the snack bar to see if our chances had improved at all. Spoiler alert: They hadn't.

In the meantime, Will had apparently been scanning the lobby for some help in the form of a security guard – or any cinema employee, I suppose. He nodded, which I, of course, took to mean we'd be fine.

"That guy over there looks like he might be a security guard," he said, motioning to a somewhat big guy stationed right near the main entrance.

Will tried waving the guy over to us, but I think there was a little too much going on for him to notice. For instance, there were a couple of older kids having themselves a candy fight, I think. Believe me, it was just like it sounds. They'd spent their money – or their parents' money – to fill their bags with candy, and then there they were, emptying them all over the carpet just like that. They were just firing them at one another like they were having a snowball fight – only with Sno-Caps instead of snow*balls*.

I could tell he didn't want to leave his post, but they were really making a mess of the place, so he didn't have much choice in the matter. Imagine that. The older kids were the ones acting up while a couple of ten-year-olds like us were doing what we were supposed to be doing – for the most part anyway. I'm sure it looked like we were trying to swipe the glasses to anyone who didn't know the truth – as bizarre as it was. By the time he'd gotten within ten feet of them, they slunk off. They certainly left their evidence there though. People were walking all over it, getting it stuck to their shoes and whatnot. For some kids, it seemed like the older they got, the more of a pain in the neck they became. I bet that security guard would agree with me. I tried getting his attention before he returned to his spot by the entrance, but he apparently didn't see me *or* hear me. It might have had something to do with the fact that our tormentors were just about surrounding us by that point.

Their faces were terrifying. I had never seen eyes so sunken in. I wasn't sure how they did it. It was almost like their head was trying to swallow them. And, it wasn't just their eyes that bothered me. Their whole face was in rough shape. I couldn't see color anywhere. Even the sickest of people usually have a little bit of color. Not them though. They had no color to them. No life. This combined with the swallowed-up eyes scared the bejesus out of me. I was too scared to be impressed with their make-up talent. I mean, they were artists – and a little creepy. Make that very creepy.

"Is it just me or do they look just like the ones from the movie?" Will asked.

Now that he mentioned it, they did look an awful lot like the ones walking off of the screen at us. In fact, one of them looked nearly identical to the one I thought for sure was going to finish off the hero in the final scene. He was wearing the same outfit and everything – overalls with a plaid button-up beneath them. It was then that something dawned on me.

"I bet these guys went to see it last weekend, and it was so good that they're back for more," I said. "Maybe they liked it so much that they wanted to go as their favorite character this time. People do that sometimes."

What a relief. I finally had a reason to smile again.

"I guess so," Will said, not altogether convinced. I could tell he wasn't so sure. "Still, who has a favorite zombie? I mean, it's not like they give them any lines or anything."

He was right. I guess there wasn't really anything that made any of them stand out. In fact, they're hardly ever in more than one scene.

We strode towards them, nice and calm with our hands at our sides. I didn't want to make any sudden movements, and I'm guessing Will was thinking the exact same thing. These people were acting strange enough already. We didn't need to give them any more of a reason to bother us.

"Should we take our costumes off?" I asked, thinking that maybe they were only drawn to us because we seemed to be as caught up in it as they were.

"Maybe," he answered. "Yeah. Let's give it a shot."

I quickly pulled my tattered shirt off. I didn't mind. Truth be told, I was sort of swimming in it anyways. After all, it was my dad's. It was an old one he no longer wore on account of he'd outgrown it. It was "a little tight around the belly." These were his words, not mine. I had a tee shirt on underneath, so I was fine with taking it off. I did have to leave my ripped-up jeans on, though, since I had nothing but underwear underneath them. Fortunately, a lot of the older kids had rips in their jeans, so I didn't feel too weird about having to walk around in them. Will was pretty much in the same boat as me. We definitely lucked out.

"My dad probably doesn't want this back, right?" I asked, balling up his shirt. "I mean, it's all ripped and stuff. I might as well toss it."

Having said that, I just went ahead and stuffed it into a nearby trash barrel. Will followed suit, even though his shirt looked like it could have been cleaned up as good as new. We copied each other often. I guess it was his turn to copy me.

He grabbed us a few napkins from a nearby counter.

"What are those for?" I asked.

"The make-up," he replied, and then began wiping it from his face. Within seconds, it no longer looked like a dead guy's face. He tried once more to remove the glasses, but it was no use. They weren't going anywhere. It was so frustrating.

I copied him. We then tossed the napkins in with our shirts and made for the exit.

We tried sliding on by them, but one of the larger ones suddenly reached for me with both arms. He legit tried to scoop me up into a bear hug. At least, that's what it looked like he was doing. The smaller one beside him, who I figured was his girlfriend, tried pulling the same stunt with Will. Neither of them was successful. We dropped to our knees and scrambled through their legs – right through the wickets as my grandfather used to say.

By that point, we'd already made a mini spectacle of ourselves, so we made a beeline for the main entrance. The sooner we got to his mom's car the better. On our way past the security guard, I was pretty sure I heard him shout something about our glasses; but, hey, the way I saw it, they'd have to chalk these two pairs of glasses up as a loss. As much money as they must have made off of that movie, I was sure they could afford it.

We pushed our way through both sets of double-doors and practically stumbled out into the street. The crosswalk was right there, but, still, it was dangerous. That was how quickly we got through those doors.

4

_____

WE COULDN'T SEE his mother anywhere. It didn't help matters any that there were people *everywhere* out there. Even though it *was* a mall parking lot, it still seemed like there were an awful lot of them out there. I mean, you'd have thought the Christmas rush had already begun, or even Black Friday for crying out loud.

Once I reached the conclusion that his mom probably hadn't arrived yet, I started to people watch. I normally reserved this particular hobby for when we were at the food court filling up on free samples, but this was as good a time as any to have myself a looksee. Thank goodness I did, too. Otherwise, I might not have noticed that it wasn't actually *people* I was watching. I'll say it. They were zombies. As crazy as it sounds – and believe me when I tell you I know exactly how crazy it sounds – they looked like the honest to goodness real thing. These definitely weren't moviegoers roaming around, and I started to think the others weren't either. Just what was going on here?

"I don't see your mom *anywhere*," I said, growing more nervous by the second. "Do you?"

Will, too, was visibly shaken. All he could do for the time being was shake his head and mouth the word *No*. I'd say he was just above useless right then. In fact, I probably could have pushed him over with little more than my finger, or at least thrown him off balance. That's how frozen in place the poor kid was.

I did the only thing I could think of. I snapped my fingers right in front of his face. At first, I was a little hesitant to do so because I wasn't sure whether or not it should be handled like one of those sleep walker scenarios where if you wake them up they lose their mind or something along those lines. I never know for sure if there's any truth to those things, but I figured I'd take a shot and hope for the best. Even if he did go a little crazy over it, he probably would have thanked me later – especially if it meant he wouldn't end up zombie food. Besides, we didn't have much time. Just like the ones in the theater, these zombies seemed to only have eyes for us. They were ignoring everyone else.

"Why *us*?" I shouted, before grabbing hold of Will's arm and dragging him down the sidewalk. We headed for a mall security cruiser I noticed parked out in front of the garage.

Once we reached it, we were instantly hit with some more bad news. Nobody was inside. It was empty except for a still steaming cup of coffee in the cup holder and a folded newspaper on the passenger seat with a pen resting upon it. Whoever was on duty that day had a crossword puzzle on his or her agenda.

"Where is he?" Will asked. "You don't think they got him, do you?"

He might have been on to something, but I didn't want to jump to any conclusions. After all, if they could grab a mall cop in broad daylight, then a couple of scared ten-year-olds wouldn't put up much of a challenge.

"We should get inside," he suggested, and then opened the passenger side door.

I quickly swatted his hand away and slammed the door shut.

"Are you out of your mind?" I asked. "We'd be a couple of sitting ducks in there. No. What we need to do is get the heck out of here."

"Okay," he agreed, and then hurried down the sidewalk ahead of me. I was glad we were on the same page. Then again, he never did like it when he had to make a crucial decision. He definitely didn't like the pressure – not that any kid in his right mind would. That should go without saying. Anyways, this was certainly one of those times he must not have minded being a follower.

I kept stealing glances at the parking lot as we walked. He was doing the same. Of course, he was probably looking for his mom, whereas I was busy weighing our chances of getting out of this in one piece. It didn't look good considering there were zombies literally everywhere. This was ridiculous. Some of them had even stepped up onto the sidewalk just ahead of us coming from the opposite direction.

"O-M-G," I muttered under my breath. "I really don't see a way out of..."

Before I could finish this thought, I noticed the one spot that didn't appear to be infested with the undead yet. It was a loading dock for Reynolds' Department Store. One of their delivery trucks must have recently pulled away because the door to the dock hadn't been lowered yet. We needed to get to it – quickly. Two circumstances weren't working in our favor; the first being that this window – or rather door – of opportunity would surely be closing soon, and the second being that the zombies coming towards us were also fairly close to the loading dock.

"See that loading dock over there?" I asked, motioning to it.

"Yeah," he answered.

"Well, get your butt over there," I ordered. "And, don't slow down for anything."

He shot me a confused look.

"*Just go!*" I shouted, and then broke off into a sprint.

He followed suit. Granted, I didn't know for sure until we got over there because I never once looked back to check. I did, however, hear his footsteps behind me every step of the way; that was good enough for me.

I took a sharp left just before one of the zombies could head me off at the pass. It was *way* too close for comfort, if you ask me.

The closer we got to the loading dock the more I realized just how high it was off of the ground. We were never going to get up and inside without some serious teamwork.

"Here's the plan," I started to say, in between pants. "When we get there, I'll give you ten fingers, okay? And then you can pull me up. How does that sound?"

He was panting too much to form any sort of a response just yet.

"Sounds good to me," he said, shortly thereafter.

The only part of the plan we hadn't anticipated was the part that left yours truly standing in a puddle for as long as it took me to boost him high enough. It must have rained the night before. Of course, with all that had gone on, I couldn't remember for sure. This was understandable, I guess.

We fell short the first time, which kind of annoyed me more than it did him. I honestly wasn't convinced he'd given it his all. Either that was the case or he'd underestimated just how difficult the task at hand was.

"I missed," he said, not sounding too bent out of shape over it. "Try to get me a little higher this time."

Unbelievable. I wanted to drop him backwards right into the puddle, but something like that would have only slowed us down. Besides, there was no way I was getting up there without his help.

"Look, you'd better get it this time," I grumbled. "Because my sneakers are *soaked*."

I stole a quick glance back towards the parking lot. A few of the zombies must have seen us because they were making their way down the ramp to join us. They were slow-moving, but they'd be there soon enough.

"And they're coming now, so get your butt up there!"

This was apparently all of the motivation he needed. I felt his sneakers finally leave my hands, and then I heard them scraping their way up the cement wall. In the meantime, I couldn't take my eyes off of those monsters. *Man!* I never thought I'd be running from legitimate monsters.

"Okay," he shouted from above. "Give me your hands."

"Gladly," I said, and then threw them up there like I was the victim of some stick-up. I think it's safe to say I'd seen one too many movies. Granted, all of the movies in the world couldn't have prepared me for any of this – not by a long shot.

Before I could brace myself for it, he grabbed hold of my hands and pulled so hard I thought for sure he was going to break my wrists or something along those lines. He was a lot stronger than I had remembered. Then again, he might have had a little of that love adrenaline going. After all, we *were* practically brothers.

Anyways, my stomach banged off of the wall and then scraped across the edge. It hurt like heck, but it beat what could have happened to me, I figured.

I jumped to my feet and watched as he started to pull the rope attached to the door down. He was struggling with it though. I guess a lot of that strength had been drained out of him. So, like any loving brother would do, I grabbed onto the rope, too, and we were able to pull the door shut. Then, I locked it from the inside, keeping us safe for the time being – or so we thought.

5

THERE WAS no one left in the receiving department – which is where all of the merchandise ends up before it's put on the sales floor. I only know that because my uncle worked in a department store. He was always trying to talk to me about his job at family cookouts, but I doubt there were many ten-year-olds who wanted to learn about the ins and outs of a department store. I was no exception. Anyways, the guys in the receiving department must have gone on break. Imagine taking a break while a zombie outbreak was going on? Actually, come to think of it, I shouldn't have been too annoyed by this. After all, it probably worked in our favor. Had they been aware of it, I'm guessing they would have pulled that door shut and locked it by the time we got down there. Who knows? They might have even boarded it up just to be on the safe side. Yup, no doubt about it, we lucked out when they took a break.

We dilly-dallied a little too long down there, if you ask me. In fact, we didn't even make our move up to the ground floor until after we saw one of their hands trying to force its way beneath the door that prior to that had seemed pretty secure. We knew the door was locked. What we didn't know, however, was whether or not these things were strong enough to barge their way in regardless. I was worried that zombie strength might have even trumped brotherly love strength.

The first department we found ourselves in was children's clothing. Of all the luck. I wasn't a fan of clothes shopping at all. Even without zombies roaming around, back-to-school shopping with Mom was a nightmare. I could only imagine how much worse it would have been with a bunch of *them* tossed into the mix.

Unfortunately, I didn't have to rely upon my imagination much longer. The first wave of them emerged from behind some fixtures in the toddler section. This really frightened me. Not because they were close to us, but because there were little kids around. The zombies were pretty much closing in on them, and there was nothing I could do about it. I'll admit it. I was too chicken to really do anything about it.

Those poor kids, I thought. I mean, their parents were right there, but they didn't seem to be paying close enough attention to them. Not close enough for me anyways.

I went to cover my eyes once the zombies got right up next to those kiddos, but it was all for naught because they surprisingly maneuvered their way right around them as though they weren't even there. They must have been off limits. The zombies appeared to have a conscience, after all. This was news to me. Of course, the more pressing news was that they were still headed our way, and I doubted we'd be as lucky as those youngsters.

"Oh, to be a little kid, again," I said.

"No kidding," Will said. "They completely left them alone. When does *that* ever happen?"

"Pretty much never," I answered.

Granted, this *was* the first time something like this had ever happened, so I wouldn't say we were experts on the subject. We *had* seen three or four zombie movies between the two of us, though, so we had a pretty good idea.

Not wanting to waste any more time on this, we took off down one of the aisles. We ended up just outside the dressing rooms.

"Come on," Will said, hustling into one of the dressing rooms.

"No!" I shouted. "We can't go in there. It'd be just like getting into the security car. We'd be trapped. Only it'd be worse because we wouldn't be able to keep them out."

He stepped out of the dressing room and trudged on back to me. I could tell he was a little miffed at me. I might have been coming off a little bossy. I was just trying to keep us alive a little longer. My bad.

"Okay," he begrudgingly said. "Then, what *is* the plan?"

Honestly, I didn't have one prepared, but, even on this short of notice, I felt I could top hiding out in a dressing room. I looked around the department store, and it suddenly dawned on me.

"Quick," I began, "let's get up on those tables there and strike a pose. They'll think we're mannequins like the others. Just, whatever you do, *don't move.*"

"That's actually not a bad idea," he surprisingly admitted. I think he was even a little surprised he agreed so readily. "It'll at least buy us some time until we come up with another plan."

You'd have thought I was standing on one leg I moved around so much up there. I think you probably would have, too. For starters, it wasn't the sturdiest of tables. Secondly, we were surrounded by zombies not long after we got up there. Perhaps the dressing room would have been a better option. I don't know. I suppose it's easy to say that now. Honestly, the only thing keeping me from apologizing to Will and admitting he was probably right was that I didn't want to draw any unwanted attention to us even though it seemed like they knew for a fact we were there. I hoped Will didn't think I was simply being stubborn. I wanted to be clear with him later on, but we just had too much going on and I eventually forgot. He probably forgot all about it himself by the time we had both jumped from the table.

He was the first to jump. I didn't even know he was planning on it. Not only was the plan to remain motionless, but I figured it was a given we'd be staying up there until they were either on their way or trying to pull us down from there. Neither had taken place, but there he was soaring through the air, leaving me behind on an even wobblier table than before.

"What are you doing?" I asked.

He simply stared at me in disbelief for a few seconds.

"What am *I* doing?" he asked. "What are *you* doing? You need to get down from there."

I quickly glanced down to find three pairs of undead arms reaching for my legs. They soon had the table surrounded. Stepping down was no longer an option, and I knew I wasn't athletic enough to make the leap Will had. The only way *I* was going to be able to clear them was if I used one of them for leverage. I figured I'd need to push off of one of their shoulders to get beyond them. The one standing directly between us seemed like the logical choice; he was a little shorter than the other two, but his shoulders looked pretty frail – like if I were to put any kind of pressure on them, I'd end up crashing right through him to the floor.

I figured, what the heck? I knew what I had to do, and I knew the risks if I stayed up there any longer. I readied myself to use his right shoulder for a stepping stone. Will kept nodding at me as if he knew just what I was planning on doing. Even though he most likely wasn't attuned to my plan, his nodding was all the reassurance I needed. I went for it.

"*Woo hoo!*" I shouted, as I nervously stepped up onto his shoulder. A maneuver like this was so far out of my comfort zone it was ridiculous.

To this day, I'm not sure why I shouted *that* of all things. The only time I normally shouted that was on a steep roller coaster or some other crazy amusement park ride. I'm guessing the adrenaline triggered it.

I completely missed his shoulder, by the way, which makes absolutely zero sense to me since my sneaker was literally coming right down on it last I checked. Then again, maybe I did get it. It might have just been so frail that I busted clear through it.

I didn't have time to find out for sure. A couple of them had already turned towards me. The others stood there in stunned silence. Well, maybe they were stunned. I don't know. Hard to tell. I mean, can you still shock the undead? Didn't seem likely. They must have just been oblivious to me once I was out of their line of sight. I'm guessing the other two might have heard me land, and that's why they turned. That happens in the movies sometimes.

I wasted entirely too much time figuring this all out in my head. While I was jogging my memory for comparable movie moments, one of them was busy reaching for my leg. Quick as anything, I clumsily tried getting to my feet. Believe me when I tell you it was ugly. Have you ever seen footage of a fawn trying to stand for the first time? Well, it was like that, but only if you strapped a pair of roller skates on the fawn's hooves and fast-forwarded the video clip.

Anyways, he grabbed hold of my pant leg just as I was getting to my feet. I panicked. I tried to pry my leg free, but I was getting nowhere for the first few seconds. There was the occasional sliver of freedom, but those slivers never lasted long. One time, I could have sworn I heard the fabric of my jeans tear – almost like it was caught up on something. Normally, I'd have been upset over it; but, if it meant I'd be free of his grasp, then he could tear those jeans all he wanted. I just didn't want to be running around the store in my underwear. I'd have never lived that one down.

Eventually, he let up just long enough for me to tear myself free. I felt a draft down near my ankle, so I knew my jeans were ruined. Mom would be pissed, but, at least, she'd still have a son to get pissed at.

Will and I took off down one of the aisles, and continued on right out of the children's department.

I kept trying to check on the zombies, but Will called me on it every time.

"Stop looking back there!" he shouted. "Or else you're gonna run right into a cash register or something."

He had a point. I wasn't too fleet-footed as it was. I'm talking bull in a China shop type stuff here, people. With this in mind, I had no business trying to run forward while looking behind me. In fact, it almost cost me dearly when I ended up just missing the down escalator.

"Dude!" he shouted. *"Pay attention!* If you had fallen down there,

that would've been all she wrote. You would've had a broken leg, a broken neck, and probably a bunch of other broken things."

"*Okay!*" I shouted back at him.

I sort of felt bad for snapping at him like that. That wasn't cool. He was just trying to protect me while protecting himself at the same time. That's a lot for a ten-year-old to handle. Now, I get that. To be honest with you, at the time, I think I was kind of annoyed with myself. Usually, whenever that happened, I gave other people a hard time. I was such a pain in the neck sometimes. And it's one thing to be a pain in the neck to your mom or your dad, but it's kind of embarrassing to find yourself being a pain in the neck to your best friend, especially when he's younger than you.

He slowed to a walk once we reached the electronics department. At first, I figured it had something to do with me being clumsy. Now wasn't the time to worry about me accidentally breaking a TV or a stereo or something like that. I mean, it's not like they would have made me pay for it while the store was being overrun by zombies.

I soon learned why he had slowed down so abruptly, and it had nothing to do with his clumsy best friend. It had everything to do with the police officer standing there. He had his gun drawn and everything. This was *great*, I thought. I honestly couldn't have been happier to see him.

"*Officer! Officer!*" Will shouted. "We need your help."

I nodded along.

He didn't so much as acknowledge us. He just stood there, gun drawn on whatever was in his sights. I looked over where he was aimed and found nothing but a 3-D TV. At first, I couldn't make heads or tails of it, but then I noticed there was a police stand-off scene on the TV screen.

Oh, great, I thought. The poor guy had lost it.

Sadly, *he* wasn't going to be any use to us.

"*Officer!*" Will shouted one more time.

"It's no use," I explained. "He doesn't even know we're here."

In typical Will fashion, he reached over and waved his hand in front of the poor policeman's face. And, nothing. No response. I mean, he didn't even seem to notice Will's hand, and it was right there waving side to side in front of his face.

I reached up to tap him on the shoulder, but Will quickly pulled my hand away. He looked at me like I had suddenly sprouted a second head.

"Don't *touch* him," he said. "He's got his gun out. You might make it go off."

Maybe he was right. After all, there were still plenty of shoppers around who the zombies hadn't gotten to yet. I would have felt horrible if the policeman had accidentally shot one of them, especially if it was my fault.

I turned to thank Will, and that's when I saw what he clearly hadn't seen. He wasn't aware enough of his surroundings. There was a zombie reaching for him from behind. There were so many of them that it was impossible to keep an eye on all of them at the same time.

I pulled him out of the way just in the nick of time. However, in the process, we both fell towards the policeman. I thought for sure we were going to crash right into him. In fact, I braced myself for the impact. I had my eyes closed and everything. Surprisingly, we never hit him. I hit the floor pretty hard though. He must have moved at the last second.

"That was weird," Will pointed out, as we sat on the floor at the policeman's feet – still unnoticed.

I glanced over at him to nod in agreement, but he was still staring up at the officer. He kind of gave him a once-over with a confused look on his face.

"I swear I went right through him," he said, bug-eyed. "I mean, literally, right through him."

He made an outward arch motion with his arm.

"No," I said, hoping to be a voice of reason, "you couldn't have. You must have imagined it."

"But…" he started to say, shaking his head in the process.

I jumped up and quickly pulled him to his feet. He was still so focused on the policeman that he almost fell back to the floor.

"Just forget about it," I said, steadying him. "We need to get out of here."

Luckily, this was enough to snap him out of it. Without further prompting, he broke off into a sprint, headed for the exit leading out into the mall.

6

Our first stop in the mall was the food court. More often than not, it was the highlight of our mall visit. We'd pretty much stalk the free sample ladies. What we'd do was we'd sidle right up to each of them, trying our best to look like we might actually be entertaining the idea of eating at their restaurant based solely on the taste of their sample. Four samples later from four different restaurants and we'd be on our way, feeling like we'd really pulled one over on the mall.

On this particular day, we did anything but sidle up to the first sample lady we encountered. Instead, we rushed right up to her, ripped the tray from her hands – dumping every sample in the process, and swung it towards the face of the zombie that was right on our heels. Surprisingly, he was more nimble than I'd given him credit for. You see, I'd always pegged zombies for easy targets. I figured they didn't know any better. But, once again, every zombie flick I'd seen seemingly proved useless. As a result, I mistakenly came all the way around and caught poor Will right in the shoulder.

"*Ouch!*" he yelled. "*Be careful!*"

"Sorry," I apologized, still gripping the tray with both hands. "I thought I had him."

I turned to try my luck, again, but I soon discovered he wasn't alone. Two other zombies had joined him. Before I could come up with any kind of a plan that most likely wouldn't have worked anyway, the sample lady snatched her tray back.

"*Hey!*" I shouted, glaring at her. "*I'm trying to help you!*"

"Yeah, well, the best way for you to help me is to get lost," she barked.

I gave the trio of zombies one last look, noticed they were getting a little more aggressive, and then quickly granted her wish.

"My pleasure," I said, just before hightailing it towards a bunch of tables. There were people seated all over the place. We could blend right in, I thought.

As crazy as it sounds, nobody noticed the zombies – or else they didn't acknowledge them. It was like they were ignoring them on purpose, sort of like my mom used to do to me whenever I had one of my "difficult days." Difficult days. It was a nice way of saying I was a pain in the butt. For the record, she *never* called me a pain in the butt. I'm sure she was thinking it here and there, but she never said it. I was either a pain in the neck, a *royal* pain in the neck when I really gave her a hard time, or having a difficult day when I was at my worst. Anyway, let's just say everyone there was treating the zombies like *they* were having a difficult day.

"They're not even looking at them," Will said. "How come? What the heck is going on?"

"They're probably too scared to look," I suggested. "Maybe they're thinking out of sight, out of mind."

Suddenly, a guy holding a slice of pizza nearly the size of my head took a break from eating to look at me incredulously. He didn't say a word though. After a few seconds, he just went back to eating. I think he noticed that some of the cheese and a bunch of the grease was dripping down onto his plate, and he wanted to do something about it. Waste not, want not, I suppose.

"It's too bad zombies don't eat *regular* food," Will said, scanning the area, no doubt spying all the different restaurants. I started to as well.

"How do we know they don't?" I asked. "I mean, just because we never see them eating regular food in any of the movies, that doesn't mean they don't. After all, they're never really around any food. For all we know, they'd love it."

One of them standing a few tables away did look like he might have actually tried the pizza. There might have been a glimmer of hope yet. I just wish he chewed with his mouth closed. Maybe it was a bad habit he brought with him into the afterlife. I had to stand there and watch as his teeth ground the pizza down at a snail's pace. It was disgusting. After a while, it didn't even resemble cheese, sauce and dough. It looked more like flesh and blood. Suddenly, a small bone poked out from between his teeth. I gasped. Last I checked, pizza didn't have bones.

"Well, there's only one way to find out," Will said, thankfully interrupting my gazing.

He then motioned to the guy's slice of pizza. I hated to do it to him, but, then again, it *was* an experiment that had the potential to pay off handsomely for all of us. I quickly snatched it from his hand, and, before he could say boo about it, I fired it in the direction of the zombie closest to us. He responded to it, so he had to have felt it. It looked like a direct hit. I couldn't really see where I got him, though, because it sort of blended in with his bloodstained shirt. I think it was blood anyways. All I knew for sure was he had a greasy slice of pizza on there too, now.

"What did you do that for?" the guy asked, standing up with outstretched arms and eyes wide open. "I was eating that, ya little jerk."

I simply stood there locked in disbelief. Was this guy serious? He was *still* ignoring the real problem here?

I was about to let him have it verbally, but I figured I was better off going ahead with the plan I had in mind. I hoped Will was thinking the same thing. Even if he wasn't, he'd most likely follow my lead. I was sure of it.

I grabbed a handful of fries from a nearby table and chucked them at one zombie's face. They were as hot as anything, so he couldn't have enjoyed it too much. Of course, I didn't wait around to take in his reaction, so I didn't know for sure. Instead, I just moved from table to table, arming myself and launching a food attack on the undead the likes of which had never been seen. Will joined in. We were taking back the food court – just the two of us. You're welcome, everyone. They certainly weren't thanking us then, but I thought for sure they would later. I've gotta tell ya; saving the world – or, at least, the mall – was a mighty thankless job if I'd ever seen one. I now know how poor Mr. Riley, our bus driver, felt. *Sheesh*.

Now, I can't be one hundred percent sure of this, but I'm fairly certain somebody threw their strawberry milkshake at me at one point. It just missed my shoulder. I know for a fact it wasn't Will and I couldn't picture a zombie engaging in a food fight, so it had to have been somebody whose lunch we interrupted. Who knows though? Maybe they were joining the fight. Maybe they were trying to slow a zombie down with it and I almost got caught in the crossfire. I didn't wait around to find out. I grabbed Will by the arm and dragged him out of there. I had to pull him away from the action. To tell you the truth, I think he was actually having fun – which was kind of dangerous when you really think about it.

7

WE HADN'T EVEN REACHED the information booth at the center of the mall before we had to duck into another store for cover. Let's just say it was getting a little too hairy for me out there in the open. The two stores closest in proximity to us happened to be a lingerie store (you know, underwear and bras and stuff) and A Toy for Everyone, which was basically just your average toy store. I think they only called it that so older guys who collected action figures wouldn't feel as weird about going in there. Personally, I don't know why they didn't just say whatever they were in there to pick up was for their kid for his birthday or something along those lines. It's not like anybody would have asked anyways. Nobody cares about stuff like that.

It was pretty much a no brainer for us. I mean, we avoided the lingerie store like the plague when there weren't zombies roaming the mall. The last thing we wanted to do was get cornered in there by them. An uncomfortable predicament only would have gotten worse. No thanks. We were all set. At least, I was. Can you believe I actually had to go in there with my mother once? Granted, she only ended up buying a normal pair of underwear, but still. There were plenty of other stores she could have bought a normal pair of underwear in. Some of them even had toy departments for crying out loud. I wouldn't have had to be anywhere near her. For the life of me, I don't know why she had to choose that store. Until this whole zombie infestation happened, *that* was the most traumatic event of my life. That's saying a lot.

"A Toy for Everyone, right?" I asked, just to make sure we were on the same page once again.

"Do you even have to ask?" Will replied.

Phew! What a relief. You never knew what other kids were thinking. Case in point, I'd seen some of the older kids go into that store before, and they didn't even have a girlfriend with them. I always thought it was sort of odd behavior, but I never knew where Will stood on it. After all, if he had thought it was cool, then I probably would have had to go in there with him occasionally since we were each other's wing man in just about everything. Luckily, I had successfully dodged that particular bullet.

You're probably not going to believe it, but we had the entire toy store to ourselves. This *never* happened. Normally, this would have been a dream come true. We wouldn't have had to wait for other kids to finish looking at certain toys before we could look at them. It just figured that the only time this happened for us was when we were in there hiding from zombies.

Before I could come up with any sort of a game plan, I found Will stocking up – literally. He was pulling a whole host of toys down from the shelves and stuffing them into a bag he found by the cash register.

"What are you doing?" I asked. "Have you lost it?"

"*No!*" he answered, sporting some sort of a deranged smile. "In fact, I've *found* it. Look around. We've hit the jackpot here."

"Wait," I said, covering the opening to his bag for a moment. "What are you doing with all of this? It's not like you can afford it."

I peeked inside his bag. It was filled. He took a break from looting the place to look at me like *I'd* gone mad.

"There is a zombie infestation going on, okay?" he reminded me. "That means everything is free."

He waved his hand by the entire section of shelving in front of us.

"Nobody's gonna ring us up for any of this. It's ours for the taking."

"Wrong," I said, snatching the bag from him. "We're not thieves. I don't care if there is a zombie infestation happening out there."

"I'm gonna give it all back when it's over," he said, cracking a tiny smile.

I simply stared at him, unimpressed, like a disappointed parent would. I think his poor attempt at lying offered me a glimpse into the nonsense he presented his folks with on a regular basis. No wonder he usually let me do all of the talking. He was lousy at it – possibly the worst I'd ever seen. I probably gave him the same look his parents gave him whenever he told them he was full at the dinner table until he heard they were having dessert.

"Really?" I asked, sporting a grin. "*You're* going to give all of this back once all of the zombies are gone?"

He let out a deep sigh, then hung his head low. Busted. I think the sense of urgency cut his charade shorter than it typically would have. He started digging into his bag and returning each toy to its spot on the shelf.

"Happy?" he asked, kind of snidely.

I gave it right back.

"Oh yeah," I answered, matter-of-factly. "I'm loving every minute of this. It's not every day you get to hide from *actual* zombies."

"Okay," he said, grinning. "Good point."

I was about to lay some more sarcasm on him when I noticed it was no longer just us and the employees in there. A few zombies must have dragged themselves through the entrance and past the sensors undetected. I couldn't believe it. The one thing about that toy store that bugged the heck out of me didn't even register with them – or rather they didn't register with it. Nothing about this seemed fair.

"Heads up!" I shouted, in a panic.

"What?" Will asked, and then spun around. "I didn't even hear the alarm go off."

Truth be told, it wasn't technically an alarm. This didn't matter though. I obviously knew what he meant.

"Me neither," I added.

In the time it took us to rack our brains over this suddenly miniscule detail, another handful of zombies entered the store. A few of them – the first ones to enter – had just about reached our row by then.

"*Uh-oh!*" I shouted. Things weren't looking good for us in there. At least, in the food court, we had plenty of space to meander around and plenty of people to hide behind. We had neither of these luxuries in the toy store. It's funny, but, until then, I never realized just how narrow those aisles were. It was no wonder we could never get to any of the toys if somebody else happened to be looking at them.

I took hold of Will's shirt just below his elbow and started pulling him backwards. I figured it might have been in our best interest to give the next aisle over a shot. There were only three in all to choose from, so I hoped we had the right one.

I hate to say it, but our situation hadn't improved one iota. There were two of them already on their way down that aisle, too. It was almost like they were trying to sneak up behind us. Who knew mindless zombies could be so strategic? Impressive.

"They're good," Will admitted, shaking his head in disbelief.

"Well, we need to be better then," I said, in what would have been a pretty sick movie line.

I followed this in the only way that would do when I pulled a massive water gun that looked to be half my size from a nearby shelf. Unfortunately, it was fastened to its package pretty well. It was as if they didn't trust anybody around it. I mean, seriously, even if you could get it out of the package undetected, what were the odds you would have gotten past the sensors at the entranceway? You'd have to be a zombie to pull something like that off.

It was evident there was no smooth way to free the water gun – not in a timely fashion anyways. So, I went with the Christmas morning approach and just started tearing the cardboard away from it as best I could. You see, I was of the opinion that since I couldn't take the water gun out of the equation, I might as well try taking everything else out of it. After a minute of some serious twisting, tearing, and, in some cases, even biting, I had a colossal water gun in my hands and a pile of discarded cardboard shreds and clamps at my feet. The only things left fastened to the gun were a couple of zip ties I couldn't gnaw my way through – not for a lack of trying mind you.

"*Wow!*" said Will. "You really went to town on that thing. You were like a wild animal making quick work of its prey."

I'm still not sure why, but, when I heard him put it like that, I felt a little pride. In fact, I even puffed my chest out a bit. What a clown.

Will most likely rolled his eyes at me under his glasses.

"Are you finished?" he asked. "Because we still have company."

"*Right!*" I shouted, immediately snapping out of it. "Sorry."

I quickly scanned the shelves on both sides of the aisle, looking for anything I could squirt at them. Yeah, I knew it wouldn't harm them any, but it would definitely distract them long enough for us to get out of there in one piece. At least, in theory, it would.

"It's too bad we'd have to go through them to get to the cash registers," Will said. "They're selling bottled water and sodas out of a cooler up there. We probably should have grabbed some water on our way back here. Oh well. So much for that, I guess."

Now, he tells me, I thought to myself. Actually, I suppose it wouldn't have been too fair of me to get on his case over it. I mean, he couldn't have known my plans would involve the mother of all squirt guns. After all, I didn't even know it at the time.

Fortunately, I soon learned he wasn't only good for *after the fact* ideas. He directed me to a package of bubble solution resting on the shelf behind me. It was a three pack – pink, yellow, and blue. Two girlie colors and a manly one.

"Why not?" I said, grabbing it. "It's better than nothing, I guess."

"Yeah," he quickly agreed. "I mean, it's still a liquid. And, if you're lucky, you might even be able to sting their eyes with it. Every little bit helps, right?"

I nodded. What can I say? It made sense. He was kind of sharp, when he needed to be.

It took much longer to empty the bubble solution into the water gun than I would have preferred. Part of the reason was because there were way too many bells and whistles on this thing. It had parts on there that it just didn't need, and then there were all of the decoys I had to deal with. Twice, I thought I found a place to pour the solution in, but all I really found were decorative knobs that wouldn't budge.

"*Hurry!*" Will insisted.

I couldn't really blame him for growing impatient with me. I probably would have been the same way. And, besides, he had just as much to lose if I couldn't load it in time.

"I'm trying," I said, panicking. "I just can't seem to…"

Suddenly, I found what I was looking for. I pulled the stopper out. Well, I pulled it out as far as I could anyways. Like most of the smaller, more reasonably sized water guns, this one's stopper came with one of those little, plastic anchors that made sure you couldn't get too far with it.

"*Argh!*" I bellowed, perhaps more frustrated than I'd ever been.

I tugged on it a few more times. After all, I needed to be able to get as much as I could in there as quickly as I could. This wasn't some backyard water gun fight we were talking about here where the worst-case scenario was us getting soaked and humiliated. I figured this had the potential to yield fatal results, and time could be a determining factor.

"You're wasting time," Will explained. "Just start pouring it in."

He was right. I handed him the water gun and started tearing away at the package of solution. As expected, it was far easier to get to than the water gun itself. Once I had the bottles separated, I immediately unscrewed the cap from the blue bottle, and, of course, I still wasn't in. I should have known it would have one of those silver seals beneath the cap as a last line of defense. This really was like a bad dream. Just in case, this time, *I* tried waking us up. Unfortunately, Will must have seen it coming because he ended up deflecting my pinch.

"Now's not the time for that," he said. "What's wrong with you?"

Again, he was right, and I suppose this debunked my bad dream theory anyways. Still, I did owe him a pinch, so I went for another one right away. This time around, I got him. He couldn't swat my hand away in time. Hey, the way I saw it, our chances of survival were looking slim now and if we weren't going to survive this, then I was at least going to get my revenge.

"Are you even serious right now?" he asked, clearly agitated with me. I guess he had every right. And, honestly, it seemed like forever ago he'd pinched me.

"Alright," I said. "You're right. I'm sorry."

I went to work on the solution. I tried desperately to poke my fingertip through the seal. It was no use though. It would bend, but it wouldn't break. I even sort of hooked my finger inwards to see if I could make more headway with my fingernail. Unfortunately, the result was the same – only I left a few tiny scratches on the seal this time. I was really starting to hate this seal.

"Give me it," Will finally interrupted. He was clearly agitated with my inability to do something as simple as puncturing the seal on a bottle of bubble solution.

He handed me the water gun and – before I could make heads or tails of it – he had taken the bottle and tried biting his way through the seal. He looked like a madman.

"What the heck are you doing?" I felt the need to ask.

"Improvising," he answered, with a piece of the seal still lodged in between his teeth. At least, I think that's what he said.

He finally broke through the seal and spit its remnants to the floor. Then, without any hesitation, he handed me the bottle.

"Okay," he began. "Load her up."

I nodded and frantically started pouring the solution into the water gun. We'd already wasted more than enough time. It was getting everywhere at first. My hands were getting sticky, which was even more annoying when your back's against the wall. Eventually, I got the hang of it. Truth be told, I probably could have gotten all three in there, but I held off. Once I emptied the bottle, I tossed it to the ground, pushed the stopper back in, aimed it at the zombie leading the pack, and fired. The result: nothing but bubbles.

"*Are you kidding me?*" I shouted, sending more and more bubbles into the air – hoping the first round was just a dud.

"*Dude, stop messing around!*" Will shouted. "We don't have time for this."

"You think I'm doing this on purpose?" I asked, finally lowering my weapon to examine it.

I shook it a few times, hoping this might knock loose whatever was forming the bubbles. I could hear the solution swishing around in there. Then, I tried my luck again. This time, a few tiny streams shot out and they were followed by a bunch of foam collecting at the end of the barrel. I thought we might have been onto something with this slight turn of events, but, sadly, it wasn't long before the bubbles made their presence known once again.

"This isn't working," I explained. "It's no use."

Before I could toss it to the floor, he came up with a Plan B, which I guess was pretty similar to the Plan A we had.

"You know, we can still shoot our way out of here," he said, sounding an awful lot like some sort of a bank robber from one of the old black and white detective movies my grandfather used to force me to watch whenever he'd try to make a case for his childhood being every bit as fun as mine. Now that I think of it, though, I probably would have traded with him in a heartbeat.

"*Shoot* our way out?" I asked, incredulously. "With *bubbles?*"

"Yeah," he answered, as though there were nothing about this that should have needed questioning.

"But…" I started to say before he cut me off.

"Trust me," he continued. "Just empty the whole thing or, at least, as much as you can right into their faces. Then, when they can't see anything, we'll scoot right by them and out the door. What do you say?"

I wasted no time. In fact, instead of taking the time to answer him, I just started firing away. Within seconds, the air was so thick with bubbles that I could barely see Will, which made sense since he was no longer beside me.

I pulled the trigger a few more times just to be on the safe side. That was it, though, because the longer I waited, the clearer the air grew between me and the zombies. I gently placed the water gun on the floor instead of simply dropping it. I didn't want to chance them hearing it land just in case they could figure out I was suddenly defenseless.

"Well, here goes nothing," I said, and then crawled through the wickets of the undead.

Once I was sure I had safely made it by them, I stood and made a mad dash for the exit, cursing the bottled water as I ran by. Will did the same. Well, maybe he didn't go to the lengths of cursing the bottled water, but he did make for the exit in a hurry. The last thing I heard was the alarm sounding. I had triggered those sensors for the last time. Hurrah.

8

"Nobody's gonna believe us without any proof," Will explained.

Proof? Why did we need proof of this? After all, the way I saw it, the proof was all around us. You couldn't miss it. I didn't even have to ask him for an explanation. He must have seen it on my face.

"So we can show the police when we get out of here. Duh."

I could have checked him right then and there by pointing out the security cameras that were just about everywhere, but I was a little more concerned about the four zombies coming our way. Either Will hadn't seen them yet or he'd gotten way too used to them. The nearest store to duck into for cover was one of those photography studios that always seemed a little out of place in a mall. The place was packed though – mostly with families by the looks of it, so they must have been doing something right. Shows how much I knew.

"It's too bad we don't have a phone," Will continued. "If we did, we could have been snapping pictures of these things left and right."

Snapping pictures? If we had a phone, I would have been *calling* the police instead of collecting evidence for them. *Sheesh!*

"Well, we may not have a phone," I replied, "but, we do have the next best thing for taking pictures. We have a photography studio."

I motioned to the studio, but he only gave it a dissatisfied look. I could tell by his pout.

"It'll have to do, I guess," he said, with a sigh.

I rolled my eyes. Fortunately, he couldn't see my reaction. He'd have just thrown some sort of a fit, and I honestly didn't have time to deal with that nonsense.

The scene in the studio – if you could even call it that – was so different from the one we'd left out in the mall. We found mothers brushing out the tangles from their daughters' hair and fathers straightening their sons' little clip-on bow ties. Meanwhile, every last one of the kids looked miserable. I had to hand it to them though. As bored as they looked, they didn't notice the craziness going on out in the mall. If I were their age, I'd have been clawing away at my father's legs, trying desperately to climb up into his arms. Aw, who am I kidding? I probably would have even tried it at my age. He would have been embarrassed as all get out, but it would have been a price I was willing to pay.

Once inside, we looked all around for a camera that wasn't in use. Unfortunately, since it was so busy, we came up empty-handed. I doubt they would have let us borrow one anyways. They probably all cost like a thousand bucks.

"*Hey!*" Will shouted. "There's one they're not using. Grab it, and let's get out of here."

I stared at it for a long moment, which I think was even longer for Will. He was so impatient, and I just wasn't in any rush to steal a thousand-dollar camera – or any camera for that matter.

"What are you waiting for?" he asked. "Grab it."

Meanwhile, all he had to do was stand there in between me and the register stand, sort of shielding me. Well, let's just say he was doing his best to shield me. When you're a ten-year-old kid with a ten-year-old body, you can only take up so much space.

"Fine," I reluctantly agreed, and then made my way over to the still unattended camera.

I grabbed hold of it, only to discover that it was clamped to a tripod. I tried to wiggle it free, but that sucker was really on there. It wasn't budging.

"Give it a little elbow grease," he suggested from behind me.

I was jittery and sweating profusely to boot. I mean, this honestly had disaster written all over it, and I was in too deep to back out now. Think about it. My fingerprints were all over that camera. Needless to say, I panicked.

"Excuse me, young man?" a voice boomed from behind me. Okay. Maybe it didn't boom exactly, but it did startle the bejesus out of me. I really didn't want to see who it belonged to. I knew I didn't recognize it, and that was enough to worry me. It sounded an awful lot like a manager's voice. Yup. It definitely had that managery feel to it.

I pretended not to hear him, but I probably should have known that wouldn't be enough. It's kind of like when Mom used to shout from the other room that I needed to clean my bedroom. More often than not, I'd pretend I didn't hear her, but she'd always just step into my room, looking peeved that she actually needed to take that walk down the hallway to entertain my charade, and tell me to get cleaning or else no video games. Oh, and she always made sure to diagnose me with "selective hearing" before she left. It certainly didn't help my act any that I could just about always hear her discussing our vacation plans with my dad with their door closed and the TV turned up. I think she was on to something with that selective hearing business.

Eventually, the guy tapped me on the shoulder. It was time to face the music. To my surprise and relief for the time being, it wasn't the studio manager. In fact, it wasn't any of the employees. It was some guy and his family. They looked like they needed their picture taken. At least, the father and son looked ready for it. The mother, on the other hand, was busy getting the last few snarls out of her daughter's hair.

He handed me a sheet of paper that I only pretended to read. There were columns, numbers, and their name and address.

"Where would you like us?" he asked.

"Huh?" I asked, not entirely sure what he was getting at.

"For the picture," he added. "Where would you like us to stand?"

"Oh, um…"

I stared at the backdrop for a moment, and then shifted my focus to the area in front of it. There was all this old-fashioned furniture sitting there. For instance, they had a rocking chair that looked none too comfortable, a huge trunk that looked like it could have been holding just about anything, and some old-school toys that I didn't think they even sold anymore. This was the kind of picture I'd have never gone along with had Dad suggested it. I would have put up a pretty good fight.

"Well, I guess *you* can sit in the rocking chair," I began, sort of painting a mental picture of what I wanted as I spoke. What do you know? Maybe I did make a pretty decent photographer. "Then, *she* can sit on the trunk, sort of looking over her shoulder at you."

I brought her over to the trunk and positioned her how I wanted her. He, in the meantime, had taken it upon himself to just plop right down in the rocking chair.

"Then, you two—meaning the kids—can just sit on the floor at your dad's feet, playing with the toys. Don't look at me, though, because it won't look as good. Sound good, everyone?"

They all seemed on board with it.

As crazy as it sounds, I got so into it that I pretty much forgot all about the zombies roaming around the mall. To be honest with you, the only thing that snapped me out of it was the fact that I couldn't snap any photos of the family. That is to say I couldn't really figure out the ins and outs of this expensive-looking camera. It wasn't like snapping a few selfies with Mom's phone. Far from it, in fact. This was the real deal – an honest to goodness photographer's camera.

I think I almost had it when Will suddenly grabbed my attention from behind.

"*What the heck are you doing?*" he asked. "*Just take it already!*"

"*Hey, listen!*" I barked, turning to face him. "I'm not going to rush it. I'm trying to capture a lasting memory for these nice people. Now, please move because I think you're messing up my lighting."

"Seriously?" he asked. "I meant just take the camera; not the picture. What *are* you doing?"

What was *I* doing? What was *he* thinking? That's more like it. I mean, he sounded like he wanted to be out there with them. And for what? So he could get a few pictures of them? Talk about crazy. At least, one of us was using his head.

I shifted my focus back to the task at hand. I played around with a few of the buttons and knobs at the back of the camera. It certainly didn't help matters that I still had those dang glasses on. I tried once more to force them off. No luck. At one point, a flash went off, so I pressed the last button I remembered pressing, and wouldn't you know it. Success.

"Okay, everyone, I figured it out," I announced.

Naturally, they were all a little confused by this. They even looked to one another and shrugged. Then, they looked back at me. The father opened his mouth to say something, but I didn't really give him the chance to say whatever was on his mind.

"*Smile!*" I shouted.

I think *I* was more excited about this family portrait than either of the parents. I mean, I was starting to feel like a real pro up there.

"*You*, the son," I said, trying to get his attention, "you're looking right at the camera. I thought I told you not to."

"But you just told me to smile," he whined. And, make no mistake, it was whining.

"Are you talking back to me, young man?" I asked. My mother had apparently come out of me, and I just let her stay out there for a while. "Let's get this straight. I won't have anyone sassing me in my studio."

"What?" Will asked, interrupting me yet again. "First of all, this isn't *your* studio. Okay? And, secondly, we…"

He suddenly stopped talking like the cat had gotten his tongue. My guess was he knew he was wrong. I didn't mind too much. If anything, his little interruptions were just a test to see if I had what it took to work through distraction after distraction. I'm pleased to report that I was doing a bang-up job.

"We what?" I asked, playing along. I had to. I didn't want to have to deal with any further interruptions. Enough was enough.

"We have company," he answered.

I quickly spun around to find a few zombies dragging themselves into the studio. I panicked, as did Will.

"Okay then," I blurted out, as I turned back to the family. "Shoot's over, folks. It came out great. We'll send you a copy in the mail."

"But..." the father started to say.

"It's okay," I replied, cutting him off. "It came out awesome. You just need to move it along because it's time for my break. Now, get going."

Even though they were still plenty confused, they stood up and shuffled along towards the register stand. We, in the meantime, looked all over the studio, hoping an idea would just jump right out at us. That was when I noticed the huge trunk just sitting there, not being used. It wasn't the safest of places to hide because we'd basically be stuck in there until this all blew over, but it was pretty much our only option at that point.

"*Quick!*" I shouted. "Into the trunk. That should buy us some time while we figure out our next move."

Will must not have had a better idea because he went along with it like right away. Who knows? It might have been the authority in my tone. I suppose I could chalk it up to my all too brief stint as a professional photographer.

We pushed the lid up together, forcing the trunk open. Then, we climbed in and gently allowed it to shut. We didn't want to make too much noise – which it most likely would have if we had just let it fall. The last thing we needed was for a bunch of zombies to have us trapped in a trunk, with no means of escape.

It worked like a charm...for like two or three minutes. I will tell you this, it wasn't nearly as roomy in there as it looked from the outside. To give you an idea, let's just say avoiding one another's personal space wasn't really an option. Not even close, in fact. And, even though he didn't say so, Will must have hated every minute of it. You see, he hated it when people invaded his "bubble," as he called it. Well, to be fair, I think his mom might have called it that and he just sort of went with it. She was a child psychologist or something like that. I don't know. All I know is she worked at the school, and she was always helping kids out when they threw tantrums. I'm guessing she had plenty of practice with Will. I can say that because we were best friends.

"How are you doing over there?" I asked, just trying to put him at ease as best I could. He wasn't complaining about where we were, but I knew him well enough to know he was on the inside.

"What do you mean by *over there?*" he asked. "I'm *right here,* practically in your lap."

Yikes. I guess I shouldn't have brought it up. I really needed to think these things through.

"Sorry I asked," I said. "Hopefully, we'll be out of here soon."

"I hope so," he replied. "Maybe I should take a peek."

That wasn't such a good idea. Not so soon anyways. I sincerely doubted the coast would be clear that quickly. I mean, they had only just entered the studio when we climbed in. Those jokers moved at a snail's pace as it was. Not to mention the place was packed wall to wall with potential victims.

"What I don't get is why no one is screaming out there," he said. "It makes no sense."

"Maybe they're in shock."

He nodded, though I'm not too sure he bought this as an excuse. He kept looking back and forth between the lid and the floor of the trunk. I could tell he was going to look out there regardless of how I felt about the idea, so I just motioned to the lid. He nodded, once again.

"Okay," he said. "Here goes nothing. It's going to be quick, and then I'll close it."

He cracked it open. Then, just as quickly, he let the lid fall shut. Make no mistake, he definitely didn't ease that sucker back down.

"*Dude!*" I began. "What are you doing? Way too loud."

"Sorry," he apologized. "I panicked. There's one like right there."

He pointed towards the side of the trunk we were facing. I froze. I immediately regretted giving him the go ahead. *Argh!* I had only myself to blame at that point. What was I thinking? He might not have done it if I hadn't shown my support. Ah, who am I kidding? He'd have done it anyways. He was the type of kid that once he had an idea in his head, you weren't going to talk him out of it. It was one of the things I normally liked about him. This wasn't one of those times.

"What do you think we should do?" he asked.

I shushed him for a couple of reasons. The first was he was talking like he wasn't hiding from something standing about a foot away from us. The second was I needed to concentrate, and it was already hard enough coming up with our next move. If we made a break for it right there and then, we might have had to go through the zombie – or zombies. We probably would have been faster than them, but, if you asked me, it wasn't really worth the risk. After all, you can outrun a quicksand pit, too, but that doesn't do you any good if you run right into it.

"Let's just stay put for now," I suggested. "Maybe he didn't see you."

I shrugged my shoulders, and he did the same. As if on cue, someone started knocking on the lid. I panicked and quickly looked all over for something to hold onto, in case he figured out how to open the trunk. You never know. My grandfather used to tell me that even a blind squirrel could find a nut occasionally. It's funny what you remember when you're in that much danger. I wonder if that's what people mean when they say your life flashes before you when you think you're about to die. Makes sense, I guess. I mean, I definitely thought we were goners.

Will found an opening where the latch was, so he did the only logical thing either one of us could think of. He clamped his fingers down on it so it wouldn't open, and then held on for dear life – both of our dear lives actually.

"Thanks, dude," I said.

"Don't thank me yet," was all he said.

In an instant, the entire trunk started rocking. There must have been more of them out there now.

"*Oh man! That's it!*" I shouted. "*They've got us! We're never gonna get away now!*"

He shot me an annoyed look. Come to think of it, I probably would have, too.

"Well, we have to try," he insisted. "On three, we're gonna pop this thing open and make a break right for the door. If one of them gets in your way, then just lower your head and run right at him. He won't know what hit him. He shouldn't anyways, right?"

I nodded. I mean, it made perfect sense to me. As far as I knew, zombies couldn't think – let alone think fast.

Instead of answering him, I just started counting. "One... two...*three!*"

In a flash, we pushed that sucker open, sprang out, and took off running. We heard the manager or someone else shout something about running in the studio, but we just kept running for the door. I darted in and out between people, and I had just about avoided every zombie in there right up until I found one waiting for me in the entranceway. I suddenly remembered Will's advice: "Just lower your head and run right at him." That's just what I did. Actually, I did him one better. I closed my eyes. Surprisingly, I didn't run into anything. I made it clear into the mall, stopping just short of a hunched over and panting Will.

I THINK there might have been too many adults in the studio and not enough kids, which probably only made us stand out more.

"I think we need to go where there are more kids," I suggested.

Will looked like he was in the process of agreeing with me by way of a head nod when he pointed to a group of girls from our school filing into some store a few doors down. I didn't even glance up at the name of the place, which may have been a mistake in hindsight. Instead, we just hustled right in.

"Where are we?" Will asked. "What is this place?"

Before I noticed a sign anywhere, I saw dolls everywhere – and I mean *everywhere*. I think there were by far more dolls than people in there. And it wasn't just dolls mind you. There were clothes for dolls on hangers, jeeps for dolls, and even miniature campsites for dolls with prices I can't even repeat with a straight face. In other words, it was heaven on earth for girls. It was just the opposite for us. I wanted to leave and take my chances with the zombies.

"Today's Girl?" Will asked. "We need to get out of here ASAP. If any of the guys from school see us in here…"

He was right, but desperate times *did* call for desperate measures. Someone famous said that once.

"I'm not worried about any of the guys from school seeing us," I explained. "It's the zombies I'm worried about. Remember them?"

Before he could respond, he noticed something over my right shoulder. Make that some*one*, and, judging by his smirk, I knew whoever it was was still alive.

"You said you weren't worried about any of the *guys* from school seeing you here," he began. "But, what about the *girls*? Specifically, Rachel Jones?"

My eyes suddenly widened.

"*Rachel Jones* is here?" I asked, clutching him by the shoulders. "Where?"

Just to bring you up to speed, Rachel Jones was the prettiest girl in the world. I'm talking the *entire* world. I was convinced without a shadow of a doubt that a prettier girl couldn't have possibly turned up anywhere. And, as if you can't tell by now, I had a small crush on her. She often left me speechless. In fact, I'm fairly certain that for the longest time she thought I was a foreign exchange student who hadn't learned a lick of English in the five plus years we'd gone to school together. The only reason I thought this was because I literally couldn't make so much as a peep any time she said "Hi" to me in the hallway.

"So, what are the odds you'll finally build up the nerve to say anything to her? After all, the world's possibly going to end in the next couple of days."

I looked at him like he'd all of the sudden lost his mind.

"What are you talking about?" I asked, dumbfounded. "The world's not ending."

He pretty much offered me the same dumbfounded look. Needless to say, we were both taken aback in that instant. Then, before we could agree to disagree, he motioned to the world outside – which I'll admit didn't look anything like the one I woke up to that morning.

"Still, we don't necessarily *know* it's ending. I mean, don't you think that's just a little extreme?"

He turned to face the entranceway. I could see him look to his left and then to his right. He shook his head.

"No," he finally answered.

He might've been on to something, I remember thinking. After all, it really didn't look too promising out there.

He turned back around to discover we weren't alone anymore. I'm not talking about who you think either. The zombies hadn't descended upon us. It was worse than that. Much worse. Rachel and her friends had.

"John?" she asked. I slowly turned to face the music. First, however, I looked to see if Today's Girl had any trunks I could hide in. It didn't.

"It is you," she said, grinning away. Believe it or not, she actually seemed excited to see me there. "I couldn't tell at first because of the glasses. What brings you here?"

"Oh…um," was about all I could get out.

Then, I looked around, completely overwhelmed by the predicament, which, of course, didn't help me look any less foreign.

"He's picking something up for his kid sister," Will said, fortunately interrupting us.

All I could do was nod along. Yup. I was there picking something up for my little sister, who didn't actually exist. How pathetic.

Rachel was all smiles upon hearing this. Why, she even placed her hands on her hips and tilted her head to the side. This was my all-time favorite Rachel pose. Okay, that definitely had a creepy ring to it.

"Aw, you are *so* sweet," she said. "I've gotta tell you, not every brother is willing to be seen buying something at a Today's Girl store. I know my brother wouldn't be caught dead in here."

Yikes! Speaking of being caught dead in there, a couple of zombies were suddenly creeping up behind her as she spoke. And, as a result, I found I too could suddenly speak.

"*Rachel!*" I shouted. "*Look out!*"

I pulled her out of harm's way in just the nick of time. I tried my best to keep her safe behind me as I backed away from them. Luckily, Will had done the same with one of her friends.

"*John!*" Rachel shouted. "*What on earth are you doing? You're scaring me.*"

CHAPTER 9 | 55

I was scaring *her*? What about the zombies closing in on us? Had they done anything to frighten her? Apparently not.

I turned to steal a quick glance at her. She looked plenty nervous, and I didn't think it was the zombies giving her the willies. I'm pretty sure it was all me.

"Are you serious?" I asked. "You're telling me you aren't worried about these zombies at all?"

Unbelievable. I hadn't pieced together so much as three words in all the time we'd known each other, and, now, the first thing I had to say to her dealt explicitly with zombies of all things. Well, at least she knew I wasn't some foreign exchange student who was failing English class year after year anymore. I guess that was something.

"I'm out of here," her friend said.

"Me, too," Rachel added. "Good luck with your zombies, John."

I turned to find them walking off in the direction of the mall.

"Hmm," Will began. "They might just be on to something with this whole calmly walking away thing. I mean, they're safe, aren't they? None of the zombies went after them. I say we try it. What's the worst that can happen?"

"Oh, I don't know," I said. "We could get grabbed from behind and eaten, I suppose."

I wasn't *really* cracking wise – at least, I wasn't trying to. I was legitimately worried about this idea being an epic failure, especially since an epic failure here would most likely result in them making a quick meal of us. It did work for the girls, though, and it seemed to be working for a lot of other people, too, so I figured it was worth a shot.

"Let's just give it a shot," I finally agreed.

He nodded. Then, we simultaneously turned our backs to the zombies and nervously walked from the store as though we had stolen something. We sped up right at the end, which I'm guessing didn't make us look any less guilty. I didn't care. I just wanted to get out of there.

10

"I THINK I know why they tracked us down so quickly in there," Will announced.

This was sure to be good. At the very least, it would be entertaining. Not only did he seem to be under the impression he knew how zombies thought, but he was also under the impression that they thought at all. I had to think that just about everyone who had ever heard of zombies knew they were mindless, and here he was thinking he'd gotten inside their mind. How interesting. I decided to humor him instead of crushing his dream of being a world-renowned zombie whisperer.

"Okay," I said, purposely taking the bait, "why?"

"Because we were like the only boys in there," he said, matter-of-factly. "Of course, they found us right away," he continued. "If we're gonna hide from them, we need to go where there are just as many boys as there are girls – if not more."

"I'm game," I said, thinking there was no harm in it.

"Funny you should say that," he said. "Because I think I found just the place."

He motioned to an arcade across the way. All that stood between us and it was a photo booth. It was one of those classic ones that spit out a strip of like four or five tiny, black and white photos of you and whoever else was sitting in there. There were always like one or two you legitimately smiled for and the rest of them were wasted on goofy faces. Well, I guess if you're having fun and making memories, then it really isn't a waste. Anyways, if things got crazy on our way to the arcade (which certainly wasn't outside the realm of possibility), then we could hide in the booth. I guess you could say it was a hiding spot on the way to our next and hopefully last hiding spot.

I didn't mention our fallback hiding spot yet because I didn't want to jinx our plans. Plus, I didn't want to accidentally get inside of the zombie whisperer's head. He had to have seen it anyways. He was always a lot more attuned to our surroundings than I was, which made sense since he was always the quarterback for our backyard football games while I was the receiver, whose only instructions most of the time were to simply "get open." It's embarrassing to admit now, but anything more complicated than "get open" usually left me so confused that I couldn't even do that much.

"Okay," he began. "Here's the game plan. If anything goes wrong on our way to the arcade, then just get your butt to that photo booth. How does that sound?"

I simply nodded. Honestly, it was all I could do to ensure he wouldn't be adding to the plan. All I knew was I was going to make a beeline right for that photo booth, regardless of whether or not I saw any zombies. I'd just say I thought I saw one headed for us. Better safe than sorry, right? Instead of getting open, I figured I'd just get safe.

As luck would have it (as bizarre as that sounds), one of the zombies was in fact headed our way, and it looked as though he was going to have no problem cutting us off just shy of reaching our destination. Well, it was Will's destination mostly; mine, unbeknownst to him, was still the photo booth.

"Alright," he said. "The photo booth, it is."

"Sounds like a plan," I replied, grinning.

We almost collided on our way to the photo booth. Once we got over there, however, I was a little more patient. I even pulled the curtain aside, so he could scoot inside. I gave one last look in the direction of our zombie friend just to see how close he was, and then joined him in there. It was pretty dark, which I normally would not have liked. On this day, though, it was sort of a blessing in disguise. The way I saw it, a dark photo booth looked like an out of order photo booth, and an out of order photo booth typically didn't draw much attention, if any. It seemed like the perfect spot for us.

"Where is he?" Will asked. "Is he right out there?"

"I don't know," I answered, shaking my head. "And, before you ask, no, I'm not going to look. If you recall, it didn't work out so well for us the last time."

We might have still been in that trunk, perfectly safe, if we had just left well enough alone. But no, we couldn't do that, and now we were in this predicament as a result. Needless to say, I wasn't too eager to make that mistake a second time.

"*Hey!*" shouted a voice from outside the booth. "Are you guys going to have your picture taken or what? We haven't got all day."

You know, as cranky as that voice was, it sure as heck beat hearing a bunch of moans and groans. To be honest with you, I didn't care if I ever heard another moan or groan again in my life. In fact, the only time I wanted to hear either of those things again was in a zombie flick. Actually, who was I kidding? I'd seen my last zombie flick. From now on, it was strictly safe stuff like romantic comedies for me. Who knows? Maybe then I'd get a bunch of girls following me around instead of zombies. *Heck!* Even movies about dogs competing in the X-Games would have been a better choice than zombie flicks.

"I think I'm giving up zombie flicks," I announced.

Will simply stared at me in disbelief.

"I love your optimism," was all he said.

What kind of a crack was that? I was being dead serious, and he came back with something smart like that.

"What do you mean by that?" I asked.

"Dude, we're lucky if we see another movie again. Period."

I had had it up to here with all of his *the world is probably going to end soon* nonsense. I'll admit it, I didn't have a lot of patience when it came to stuff like that. I didn't like it when people were downers, and you didn't get much further down than thinking the world was coming to an end in the not-so-distant future.

"Do you have to be so negative?" I asked.

Suddenly, someone – or even something – slapped the side of the booth hard enough for the curtain to move. It slid open just far enough for me to catch a glimpse of the grumpy-looking customer behind us, who clearly wasn't thrown off by the out of order charade we were going for. He threw his arms up in frustration. I was on the verge of explaining myself, but it probably would have only fallen on deaf ears. I mean, it's not like he could have missed the zombie invasion taking place around him. Then again, he might have been too focused on me to even notice them, which was kind of crazy considering one of them was standing right next to him.

I tried to do the right thing when I motioned to the zombie with the slightest of head nods. I hid it as well as I could out of fear that the zombie would notice me sooner rather than later. Of course, this only seemed to annoy the guy further. The son of a gun even tapped his watch for me. *Whatever,* I thought, and then pulled the curtain shut again.

"*Oh, come on!*" he shouted. "*We have places to be, so get the show on the road!*"

I wondered why such a busy guy even had the time to take corny photos in the first place. I mean, we at least had a legitimate reason to be in there.

"What's with this guy?" Will asked, exasperated. "The louder he gets, the greater our chance is of getting caught. How do we quiet him down?"

I did the only thing I could think of in that instant. I fed that machine my last dollar. I was hoping to use it on candy, but I figured it would do us more good in the photo booth. Will, on the other hand, didn't even reach for his money. What a cheapskate. Sure. Leave it to me to save our lives with my allowance. No problem. He definitely owed me one if we ever got out of this mess.

"The next one's on you," I pointed out.

"The next one?" he asked, clearly dumbfounded.

"Yeah," I said, matter-of-factly. "It doesn't take that long to snap a few photos, and Mr. Happy out there will be expecting us to vacate the photo booth ASAP once we're finished. It'll be your turn to buy us some more time – literally."

After some huffing and puffing, he reluctantly dug his hand into his pocket and pulled out a crumpled dollar.

We were midway through our second strip of photos when I felt someone give the booth a terrific shove. I only shook my head in disappointment. Will did the same. We knew who it was, and I couldn't get over how childish this grown man was behaving. I really didn't want to have to pull the curtain aside to tell him off though. For starters, I was afraid of him. There's no shame in that, when you really think about it. And, secondly, I was afraid of zombies even more, and there was *definitely* no shame in that. So help me though, if he shoved our booth just one more…

As if on cue, another shove came. I just knew this joker couldn't leave us alone.

"*That's it!*" I said. "I'm going to say something to him. This is ridiculous."

"I don't think that's such a…" Will started to say.

I, of course, pretended not to hear him. I then proceeded to pull the curtain aside, and immediately wished I hadn't. It had nothing to do with the guy, by the way. In fact, he wasn't even out there anymore, which, of course, terrified me. I even poked my head out for a better look, but it was no use. He was gone. I was afraid they had gotten him. Maybe they too were sick of hearing him flap his gums.

"What the heck are you doing?" Will asked.

He then reached across me and pulled the curtain shut on his own. The nerve of some people. What's more was he tore part of it up top. Well, it wasn't the curtain so much as the rings holding it in place. Two of those snapped right off and fell to the floor.

Before I could re-fasten the curtain, an arm that wasn't quite alive reached into the booth followed by a grotesque head that was just as dead. All the while, the camera was clicking away. Between the repeated flash of the camera and the zombie's arm repeatedly swiping at us, we had no choice but to run out of there as quickly as possible. It's a good thing those booths came with an exit on both sides. Otherwise, we might not have made it out of there in one piece.

We hightailed it right out into the mall like a pair of deer escaping to the forest. Once we were far enough away, Will launched into his rant about me not grabbing the photos on my way out. Unbelievable.

"How come you didn't grab the photos?" he asked, looking thoroughly disappointed in me.

"Um, maybe because I wanted to get out of there alive," I said, more than a little annoyed. "Is that a good enough reason for you? My goodness."

"I guess so," he surprisingly said. I wasn't expecting him to come to his senses so quickly. It usually took him a while.

"And, besides, you didn't grab them either," I added, just to remind him that we were in this together.

"Let's put the past behind us," he suggested.

Hmm. Somebody didn't like shouldering his share of the blame very much.

"Okay," I agreed. "But, just remember that when you point a finger at someone else, there's always three pointing right back at you."

He, of course, had to try it out.

"I think it's time we head to that arcade," I said, interrupting his counting. "We've already spent too much time out here in the open."

As it turned out, our squabbling had just about gotten us surrounded by the undead. It was sort of embarrassing, if you want to know the truth. I mean, let's face it, a zombie should never be able to get the drop on you, let alone a handful of them.

"Where have I seen that one before?" Will asked, pointing directly at the lead zombie.

"Beats me," I replied. "But I'm not interested in getting a closer look. Neither are you. Come on."

I quickly grabbed hold of his wrist, and got out of Dodge, headed for the arcade. And, just so you know, I let go of it almost right away. It would have been a little weird if we had held hands the whole way.

11

THIS PLACE WAS GOING to be the perfect hideout. There were kids just about everywhere you looked. No exaggeration.

"This'll do," Will declared.

He scanned the entire room, nodding his head as he went. I too scanned it. I wasn't taking a headcount of gamers so much as searching for potential hiding spots. There weren't too many – not from where I stood anyways. Like I said, though, there were plenty of kids in there, so there didn't really need to be plenty of hiding spots. A few would do.

"Alright," I said. "I think it's time we disappeared into the crowd. What do you say?"

"Sounds good to me," he answered. "Do you think we should split up? I think it'll make us smaller targets."

As much as I didn't want to break the team up, I knew he was right. It was common sense. That must be why you see so many people splitting up in movies when they're being chased. I'm telling you, movies certainly prepare you for a lot.

I'll be the first to admit it, I was pretty picky with my choice of hiding spots. I could have and probably should have just settled for any of the handful of racing games I came across. Those were the ones

I rarely went into for the simple reason that they usually cost you up to four tokens to play. No thanks. For the same amount, I could empty a couple of rounds in Zombie Killer when Mom wasn't looking and just fall short of winning an Xtreme Motocross race. Plus, the last time I sat down in a booth, I came fairly close to being zombie food.

Still, I suppose those booths didn't look so bad once I saw Will trying to climb into one of the basketball games. I'd never seen anyone attempt that before. Granted, I'd also never seen anyone trying to hide from zombies before other than in the movies. Let the record show that I did give the skee ball machines an extra look. Hey, listen, you really couldn't rule anything out by that point. After all, it was crunch time.

One thing was for sure: I would need to think outside of the box. On second thought, perhaps this called for being inside the box. More specifically, perhaps it called for being inside the claw machine. I think that's what they're called anyways. I normally called it the highway robbery machine.

This claw machine was different though. It actually looked like a can't miss one. It was huge. Actually, everything about it was huge – the prizes, the claw, and the machine itself. It looked like a strong claw, too. I bet it could have picked up a basketball if you stuck a few in there. Maybe I went a little overboard there, but I bet it at least could have picked up a kickball.

"*Ouch!*" I heard Will shout. I knew it was his shout because he always overdid it. He could be pretty dramatic sometimes.

I looked over to find him struggling. The poor kid had gotten his ankle caught up in the netting. Even though I probably shouldn't have, I burst into laughter. He probably didn't hear me, but it was still kind of a rotten thing to do. I felt a little guilty afterwards, so I figured I owed it to him to help him out.

My good intention quickly fell by the wayside though. Well, I suppose it's more accurate to say it was pushed to the wayside by my overwhelming fear of the zombie that suddenly stepped directly in my path. I didn't think he saw Will, so that was a good thing. It bought him just enough time to pull his ankle free.

A group of little kids then entered the picture. I first noticed them in my peripheral off to my right. The zombie didn't so much as look at them. He was another one that only had eyes for yours truly. It sucks being popular sometimes.

I wasn't all that worried about the little ones since he apparently wasn't there for them. Surprise, surprise. Not only was I not worried about their well-being, but I decided I'd use them as a cover. Yup. Just as they were passing between us, I ducked down and quickly crawled alongside them until I was in the clear.

The clear, as it turned out, was right near the oversized claw machine I told you about. I ducked down beside it for the time being. I kept stealing glances over to where I left that dopey zombie, but he wasn't there any longer. He must have finally moved on to someone else. Thank goodness. Not that I wanted anyone else to get eaten, but it was kind of nice to have him off of *my* scent.

I'm not quite sure how it happened, but I somehow found myself a lot more worried now that I couldn't see him. I panicked, wondering where the heck he was and if he'd somehow gotten closer to me without my noticing. That's when I noticed the key to the claw machine dangling a few feet from my face. It was attached to a whole ring of keys. How anybody could have forgotten all of them was beyond me. Somebody who worked there must have accidentally left them in the little door on the side of the machine when they were in a hurry. I'm guessing that's where they filled it. I say little but, truth be told, it looked large enough for me to squeeze through, which naturally gave me an idea.

I scanned the area one last time, looking for the zombie and anyone who worked there. Once I determined the coast was clear, I popped the door open and crawled on in. Either it was a larger door than I had originally thought or I was smaller than I thought because I got in as quick as a jackrabbit. Yikes. Not sure where that expression came from. Probably from my grandfather. The man's native tongue was old-timey expressions, and I swear corny humor was his second language. I laughed at all of his jokes – mostly because he was old. Old people love it when you think they're funny. It's kind of a big deal for them. At least, for him it was.

I felt kind of odd just sitting in there. I mean, what on earth was I going to do if some kid walked up to use the machine? Just wave him off? Maybe I'd scare him off, which under any other circumstance would have been priceless. Yeah. I'm sure either one of those options would have gone over great with the little angel's parents. The thought did occur to me to just open the door and pull the cord out of the wall as quickly as possible, so people would think it was out of order. But I didn't really want to draw unnecessary attention to myself in case the zombies hadn't seen me crawl in there in the first place. That would have to be an idea for the back-burner for the time being.

It was so strange in there. To give you an idea of just how strange it was, try picturing this: I was sitting on what was probably hundreds of those little, colored, glass stones you sometimes find in a fish tank or in a vase if your mom does that sort of thing, and I was surrounded by all of those prizes that are nearly impossible to win. I'd never seen anyone win one of them anyways. I always figured the coins they took out of those machines at the end of the night previously belonged to suckers. I still think I'm right about that.

I started playing with a few of the prizes. Somebody had to, right? No *kid* was going to. That was for darn sure. There was a sick-looking gun that shot foam darts. You'd either need crazy luck with this claw or like a million tickets to get your hands on one. Meanwhile, you could probably pick one up at just about any toy store for like fifteen bucks – maybe even ten. This place was such a rip-off. Always had been.

I decided then and there to win one for the kids of the world. It would be a moral victory over the arcade – albeit a small one. I grabbed some action figures I found in there, ripped their packages open, and lined them up against the wall of the machine. Then, I started picking them off one by one. The problem was I got so into sticking it to the arcade that I'd completely forgotten why I was even in that machine in the first place.

A not so friendly reminder pressed his face to the glass, interrupting my target practice. Much like whenever I was in the snake house at the zoo near our house, I was *so* glad to have a pane of glass separating us. The only difference being that I was apparently the exhibit this time around.

The good thing was he couldn't shake the machine. It wouldn't even budge for him. Granted, it *was* huge, like I said. He was growing frustrated, but he wouldn't leave me be. It might have been a waste of time for him to stick around there, but something told me zombies didn't really care about that sort of thing. Either everything was worth their time or they had no concept of time. It was most likely the latter.

The one thing being stuck in there afforded me the opportunity to do, which I really could have done without, was have myself a good, long look at the zombie's face. I couldn't stop staring at his mouth for some reason. I hate to say it, but I think that reason was I could see bits of human flesh stuck in his teeth. Needless to say, I wasn't in any rush to get out of that machine. None whatsoever. I didn't want any of my flesh to get stuck in his teeth. No, thank you.

I froze once it dawned on me there was no easy escape from this one. By the time I'd have gotten my upper body through that seemingly even tinier door, he probably would have grabbed me. Even the slowest of zombies probably would have been quick enough. It was definitely a disappointing turn of events. I thought I'd found a top shelf hiding spot; it turned out to be anything but.

I snapped out of my frozen state when something slammed right off of the glass. At first, I figured it was the zombie slamming one or both of its fists against it, but then another object made a similar thud – this time leaving a tiny crack in it. I did get a good look at it this time around. It was a basketball a little on the small side. *Will to the rescue!*

"*Hey!*" someone shouted. "*What do you think you're doing?*"

Within seconds, it seemed, my zombie friend had been replaced by some dude with a name tag. His name was Marty F. Evidently, there was more than one Marty on staff.

He jumped back once he noticed me in there. I think he was just there to see how much damage Will had done with the basketballs. Let's just say I was an added bonus. Well, I suppose "bonus" makes it sound as though he actually appreciated the fact that I was in there. In reality, I'm pretty sure they frowned upon having kids – or anyone else for that matter – inside of their machines.

"What in the..." he started to ask. "How the heck did you get in there?"

I shrugged my shoulders for some reason, even though I obviously knew exactly how I'd gotten in there. I guess what it came down to was I just didn't want any of his co-workers to get into trouble for accidentally leaving the keys in the door. I figured people got fired for stuff like that all of the time. Plus, whoever left it in there sort of helped me out, even if it was only for a little while.

"Are you alright, kid?" Marty F. asked.

He definitely had a concerned look in his eyes. He probably thought I'd gone mad, which I guess made sense since I pretended not to know how I even got inside there. I would have pitied me, too. And it wasn't like I was old enough to have a driver's license yet, so he had no real way of knowing who I was other than taking my word for it. I mean, for all he knew, the crazy kid he found sitting in a claw machine was liable to say just about anything when asked who he was. He might have heard anything from President Abraham Lincoln to an alien from some planet I made up on the spot. My options were limitless. Poor guy.

I could have really messed with him, but I chose to spare him any further awkwardness. Or, at least, I tried to. Sometimes, a little awkwardness is unavoidable. I simply nodded, foolishly hoping this would do the trick and he'd return to whatever he'd been doing satisfied.

"Okay," he continued. "How's about you come on out of there then? I'll help you find your mom."

A small crowd of onlookers had gathered around him. He gave them a once-over. He might have been trying to find a match – or at least a face that looked somewhat like mine. He was a smart dude.

Truth be told, I looked a lot like my mom. There was no mistaking I was her son. She wasn't there, though, so his detective skills were going to prove useless.

"Does this kid belong to any of you?" he asked, clearly a little flummoxed.

They quickly shook their heads.

It wasn't until he began patting his pockets that he must have remembered exactly where he left his keys: in the side door of the oversized claw machine. He cautiously walked around to the side, crouched down, and gently pushed the door open. I could tell he was reluctant to stick his head right in there with me. He decided to call for me from a safe distance.

"Okay, kid, fun's over," he explained. "Come on out of there."

Fun? He thought this was fun for me? Really? Exactly which part? The part where I ran all over the place for my life? Or was it the part where I felt trapped in a glass box while a zombie peered in at me? Maybe he felt he had to say something like this since he had a bunch of mothers with him. Maybe he really wanted to let me have it with a few curse words for not only finding the keys *he'd* lost, but also using them to climb into a machine I wasn't supposed to be in. Maybe it wasn't the wisest decision in the world to play with the prizes in there. Actually, the way I saw it, he really only had himself to blame – and maybe the pack of zombies as well. I was just trying to survive. Who could blame me?

"No," I politely answered, standing my ground.

Just because he didn't curse at me, that didn't mean I was just going to crawl on out there. For all I knew, the zombie was just playing dead for the time being, waiting for me to be foolish enough to serve myself up to him. Wait a minute. Had I actually accused a *zombie* of playing dead? Lol.

"Aw, come on, kid," he whined. "Don't make me crawl on in there and pull you out."

Just so you know, there was no way that was going to happen. Let's just say Marty F. hadn't missed too many meals. Translation: The odds of him following through on that particular threat were slim to none. No pun intended. Now, I'm not poking fun at his weight, by the way; I'm merely pointing out just how empty his threat was.

Just then, one of the women braved stepping forward. She lightly tapped on the glass. I looked up to find the same kind of worried mom look that my mother usually went with. She even tilted her head to the side like Mom used to. It was sad, yet comforting. I mean, I wasn't going to cry or anything, but it was sort of an emotional moment for me.

"Um, honey, why don't you just come with me, and we'll find your mother?" she suggested. "She's probably worried sick about you."

Not really, but that's only because she probably hadn't caught wind of the zombie infestation yet. As if hypnotized, though, I slowly nodded my head in agreement. I think part of it was I also wanted to protect *her*. If the calmness defense happened to falter, then I didn't want this poor woman to get mauled – in the mall. She was too sweet, and she reminded me too much of Mom.

I crawled out past Marty F., stood up, and made my way over to her. She smiled. I instinctively gave the claw machine one last look. That was when it hit me.

"*The gun!*" I shouted, with my forehead pressed to the glass. "I need it, and I need the darts, too."

"Sorry, kid," Marty F. said, now sporting a pretty smarmy grin, "but you'll have to *win* it now, just like everyone else."

He then hooked the ring of keys onto his belt loop, and gave them a little jingle for good measure – or just to be an even bigger jerk. Take your pick.

"Now, where did you last see your mom?" the woman asked, directing me away from Marty F., who may or may not have been my newest nemesis. You'd think I wouldn't need another one. You'd think the zombies would have been enough.

"The movie theater," I answered.

"The movie theater, huh?" she replied, looking sorry she'd asked.

"She's not there though," I quickly pointed out. "She dropped me and my friend off, and his mom was supposed to pick us up after the movie."

"Wait," said some boy who had inched his way over to her side. I think he might have been her son by the looks of it. "What movie did you see?"

"*Zombies: Too Close for Comfort*," I said, practically bragging about it.

She sighed, and then shook her head. Typical mother reaction.

"Well, this explains a lot," she said.

"*Cool!*" her son shouted. "Can I…"

"Absolutely not," she said, completely cutting him off. "You're too young."

The poor kid looked so defeated.

"Aw," he groaned. "But he's…"

"Not my son," she interrupted.

She shot him the same stern look my mother probably would have gone with. It was one I'd seen plenty of times. I wasn't a bad kid. I was just a…kid. I was a normal, everyday, run of the mill kid, as far as I was concerned. Her kid probably was, too. At the end of the day, though, I guess it was a good thing we both had normal, everyday, run of the mill mothers.

She looked in and around some of the other machines in the area. Then, she hit me with it.

"This friend you told me about. He's real, right?"

What? Of course, he was real. What kind of a question was that? He was a real pain in the neck at times, but he was definitely real.

"Yeah," I said, matter-of-factly.

"Okay," she calmly said. "Then, where is he? Is he here in the arcade?"

"Yup," I answered, slightly embarrassed.

Will's current status wasn't pretty. Not in that serious, overtaken by zombies sort of way. Nope. He was trying and repeatedly failing to climb out of the basketball machine.

"That's him over there," I continued, pointing him out.

She and her son both turned towards the basketball machine. Again, she shook her head. The poor woman was probably wondering what she'd gotten herself into. I wanted to laugh at the absurdity of this predicament, but I thought better of it. I doubt she wanted to hear my laughter. Not at a time like this. She turned back towards me, looking completely dumbfounded over this crazy change in her probably otherwise normal Saturday.

"What's wrong with you two?" she asked me, point-blank. That one was right from the hip. "I mean, how did this even happen? You stuck in a claw machine and your friend stuck in a basketball game?"

I was going to make something up, so we wouldn't sound too crazy, but I figured that window of opportunity had already closed. I could see it now. I would have tripped all over my words, and she would have seen right through it. Besides, what normal reason could I give for seeking shelter in a claw machine? Sorry. Wasn't happening. I'm afraid we were all in now.

"Zombies," I said, nonchalantly. "We're hiding from the zombies."

If they wanted to pretend like they weren't roaming around everywhere, then that was fine for them. We had a different strategy though. To each his own.

"Seriously?" she asked, visibly unimpressed with me now. "You see, *that's* the problem with your generation. Everything's a joke."

She turned and marched away, mumbling something as she went. Junior hung back for a moment to mock me a little. He made sure she was out of earshot before laying into me.

"What's wrong with you, dude? You're such a weirdo."

"*Argh!*" I shouted, lunging into a pretend zombie stance. I actually looked nothing like the real thing, but it was enough to send him running. He hurried to his mother's side.

I was beaming with pride up until the little stinker gave me a sideways sneer. Just to show him I, too, could be a stinker, I dragged myself a few steps in his direction. The little punk just maneuvered around to the other side of his mother. Victory.

Now that I was no longer in hiding, I figured I should probably help Will escape the dreaded basketball game of doom. First, however, I stopped off at the Whac-A-Mole machine. It has always been my favorite old school arcade game. For the life of me, I don't know what it is. I mean, I've never even been particularly good at it. It's just so addicting. I feel the need to play it whenever the opportunity presents itself, and this time was no exception.

I was three whacks in when he joined me at the machine. I'm not talking about Will, by the way. Nor am I talking about that clown Marty F., who I definitely would have been happier to see. I'm talking about that zombie who had wandered off when I snuck off to the safety of the claw machine. He was back and looking a lot hungrier than before. Maybe it was because he was right up in my face this time around.

"*Argh!*" I shouted, which didn't faze him in the slightest. It had scared the daylights out of Junior only moments earlier, but the real deal clearly wasn't impressed with my cheap imitation.

That was when I resorted to the only thing I could think of. I took a swing at him. It wasn't with my fist though. I used the Whac-A-Mole mallet instead. I almost got him, too, but he backed away at the last second. I was kind of impressed. I didn't expect a zombie to be so fleet-footed. I took a few more wild swings at him, but came up short each time. The rope connecting the mallet to the rest of the machine only stretched so far.

"*You coward!*" I shouted. "Come here, and fight like a man...er zombie."

He didn't take the bait. He just stayed put, growling away like he was for it. In other words, he could talk the talk, but he couldn't back it up. He was all bark and no bite. I guess that was a good thing though.

I kept swinging the mallet, just to keep him at bay. After all, I figured he'd eventually get sick of not doing anything. In the meantime, Will managed to climb out of his predicament. He didn't make it very far, though, for two of the zombies had cornered him at one of the dance machines. As strange as it sounds, I nearly burst into laughter. There's something you need to know about Will. He hated those dance machines with a passion. Aside from pushing out tickets, he thought those machines were pretty much useless. Translation: He wasn't a good dancer.

They backed him right up into the machine. It didn't take long for the poor kid to run out of room. I felt bad that I couldn't get over there to help him out. My zombie didn't appear to be in any rush to beat feet. He was getting to be really annoying.

"*Beat it!*" I shouted. "*Hit the bricks!*"

I tried waving him away with the mallet instead of just swinging it at him. Believe it or not, my waving that thing around like a madman did do me some good. It got good old Marty F. to give me an earful again. He stormed over and got right in between us, with his hands firmly on his hips.

"Listen, kid," he began. "I'm starting to get really sick of your shenanigans."

The way he was looking at me, I could tell I was annoying the heck out of him. Truth be told, he was starting to make me a little nervous. Plus, you should have seen the way he stepped right in front of that zombie. It was like he didn't have a care in the world or what was left of it – least of all that some stupid zombie would attack him. He was practically standing on the zombie's foot.

"Keep it up, and I'm gonna have to kick you out," he added. "And, if you're not gonna play this game, then do me a favor and keep your hands off of it. Go find something else to do. For instance, why don't you go check out the kid on the dancing machine? I think he's going for a record."

"Seriously?" I asked. I couldn't believe my ears. Surely, he wasn't talking about Will.

"Yup," he answered, and then stepped aside. "See for yourself. He's got a whole crowd of people rooting him on over there. I've never seen anyone that good, and I've been working here for a long time. That kid's like a pro or something."

Indeed there was a crowd of onlookers over there. Will definitely had an audience. I gave one last look at my zombie tormentor, but he was nowhere to be seen. I had to admit it. He was darn good at pulling this vanishing act.

"*What's wrong with you people?*" Will shouted. "*Get out of here!*"

He was trying to save them all, but none of them seemed to take him seriously.

"I'm not going anywhere," said some kid off to my right. I recognized him from school. "He said the same thing to us in the dugout one time when he was in the middle of throwing a no-hitter. He didn't want the rest of us to jinx him by talking about it. He's a pretty intense kid. Crazy even."

Evidently, he and Will were on the same little league team a couple of years earlier. I remember the game he was talking about. Will got all the way to the second out of the last inning without so much as giving up a foul tip. Then, he accidentally threw one of the kids a meatball right down the middle and the kid ripped a liner right in between the centerfielder and the right fielder. Will blamed the kid who tried talking to him in between innings and he wasn't much fun to be around for the next week or so. The kid at the arcade was right. Will could get pretty intense when it came to certain things.

"Yeah, well, he's on pace for the record, so I'm not going anywhere either," the other kid said.

I really wanted to let them have it – verbally, of course. But, let's face it; when a kid's about to break any kind of a record, even if it's one he doesn't even know he's breaking, then it's natural to want to watch him and even cheer him on. And, these people must have really wanted to see him break it if they were willing to stick around while two zombies were standing right there.

Speaking of which, there was enough space in between them for me to get a good look at Will's dancing. He had some great moves for sure, but it was so much more than that. He was successfully navigating his way around that tiny dance floor, ducking and dodging two pairs of zombie arms every step of the way. All the while, his score was skyrocketing. If he kept this up, then the long-standing record was sure to be yesterday's news. The funny thing is, by the looks of it, Will had no idea he was on pace for the record. He was just trying to survive a zombie attack. What made this even funnier was he was easily one of the more competitive kids I knew.

He was just about ten points shy of the record when his left foot nearly slipped off of the dance floor. The crowd literally gasped, and the two boys I told you about actually got up onto their tiptoes. This was turning out to be a pretty big deal; so much so that I almost forgot about the zombies.

When he recovered his balance, the crowd just about lost their mind. You'd have thought they were going to parade him through the streets of town if he broke this record. And, still, he only had his eyes on two members of that crowd; they were as dead as the rest of them were alive.

Suddenly, the screen with the scores on it lit up like the Fourth of July. *He'd done it!* My friend Will – a kid who, like I said, hated the dancing game – broke the record for highest score on that machine. He was amazing, and he had no idea until I told him later on. I'd never seen such a huge celebration in an arcade before. It had to have been up there with the likes of the Super Bowl, the World Series, and, heck, even the World Cup. I guess people really liked that dancing game, even if their newly-crowned champion didn't.

I quickly snapped out of it, remembering why he was up on that dance floor in the first place. As the crowd celebrated with high-fives and imitations of Will's record-breaking dance moves, I wormed my way through and tapped Will on the shoulder. The zombies didn't even see me coming. It was too late before they finally caught wind of me.

"*Quick!*" I shouted. "*They're still a little distracted. Let's get out of here.*"

He gave them one last look, and then finally acknowledged the crowd gathered behind them. All eyes were on him. Maybe they were waiting for a speech or something. Who knows?

"What the…" he started to ask, clearly a little overwhelmed.

"*Look!* We don't have time for your fans," I shouted. "*We have to go!*"

"My fans?" he asked.

This information stopped him dead in his tracks. And if I didn't do something about it pronto, then he might have been dead for real – or rather undead. I grabbed his arm just like before and dragged him out of there. I'm telling you, that kid owed me big time. I didn't see any of his adoring fans jumping to his rescue.

12

WILL WAS STILL RIDING PRETTY high once we got back out into the mall. He was beaming as he ran. Not to sound too jealous, but it was kind of annoying.

"Get your head in the game, sport," I said, hoping to snap him out of it. After all, I needed him on all cylinders.

Speaking of running on all cylinders, we almost ran smack-dab into a brand-new sports car. And, no, we hadn't mistakenly run out into the parking lot. This car was sitting there all by itself in the middle of the mall.

"*Whoa!*" Will shouted, sliding to a stop just short of the car. "How did *this* get here?"

He started looking around, probably trying to make heads or tails of it all. I wondered the same. That was until I noticed a few zombies headed our way. They were pulling up the rear. They didn't look like the ones from the arcade, but there were so many of them roaming around that it was hard to tell. Plus, I guess it didn't really matter. They were all after the same thing anyways – us.

"Well, I don't know *how* it got in here," I replied. "All that matters to me is that it *did* get in here. So, let's get in, and lock the doors."

"Works for me," he happily agreed.

And, just like that, we had ourselves a sweet ride. Well, a sweet hiding spot anyways. The tinted windows were a nice bonus feature, especially given our circumstances.

It didn't take long for us to be discovered though. As a matter of fact, it was only seconds. We had literally just shut the back door and already a couple of them were at the windows, looking every bit as ugly as the others. They were trying to get a good look at us. I dove for the power lock in the front seat in just the nick of time. At least, I think it was in the nick of time. I honestly had no idea how long it took a zombie to figure out how to lift a door handle.

I swear at one point one of them pointed right at me and then at his own chest. *Yikes.* It was then that I did one of the stranger things a person probably could have done in that situation. I put my seatbelt on. I don't know why. I think it was because I panicked. And when you panic, you do some crazy stuff.

"What are you doing?" Will quietly asked. "What if we need to make a quick getaway?"

"Something tells me leaving this car isn't the best option for *me*," I said.

I could have been wrong, but he looked like he resented that statement. Come to think of it, he probably felt a little left out of whatever I had in mind.

"For both of us, I mean," I immediately added, hoping this quick edit would do.

He slowly shook his head. *Dang it.*

"But you mentioned *you* specifically," he noted. "What was that all about?"

There was no point in keeping it from him any longer. After all, if it was me they were after, then there was no need for him to stick around in harm's way.

"Well, they may not be after you," I said.

His jaw hit the floor. He practically looked angry over it. Imagine being angry over the fact that a bunch of zombies *don't* want to attack you. Hmm. We should all be so lucky. He looked at me like I'd lost my mind, but I thought a case could have certainly been made for him.

"You think they're only after you?" he asked. "Do you know how crazy that sounds?"

"I know," I agreed. "But, didn't you see how that one zombie pointed right at me and then at himself? That means he wants me all to himself."

By the looks of him, I'd say he'd clearly missed it.

"Okay," I said. "See for yourself then."

I motioned to the window, where we found the two of them in a shoving match. Now, the other one was pointing at me and then at himself. He was even tapping the glass. He was doing it with a little force, too. The sound alone was pretty unnerving. I almost had to cover my ears. Honestly, my only other option was to start humming my favorite song, but it annoyed the heck out of Will whenever I did that. In his defense, though, I normally only did it to annoy him. He hated that song, but I think it was mostly because everyone else loved it so much. I mean, it was on the radio just about every time Dad drove us anywhere.

Aw, what the heck? We could have both used a break from the craziness. We were in desperate need of some familiarity. At least, I was, even if it was the kind that annoyed him.

"Well, if they're after you, then they'll need to go through me," he said, sounding like an honest to goodness tough guy from the movies.

I was so proud of him. It was no wonder this kid was my best friend. There was no way I was going to purposely annoy him now.

It didn't take long for all of the other zombies to show up. Word seems to spread quickly with zombies. They say Great Whites can smell blood from like a mile away. Well, that's nothing compared to this. We were inside of a car for Pete's sake, and they *still* smelled us. If I wasn't too busy being terrified, then I probably would have been impressed.

They had us surrounded. There were two or three of them at every window.

"This was exactly why I didn't want to get into the security cruiser," I reminded him. *"Dang it!"*

He stared at me with this huge, ear to ear grin for a few seconds.

"What?" I asked, growing a little agitated.

"This was *your* idea," he reminded me. "*You're* the one who wanted to get into this car."

"*Listen!*" I shouted, huffing and puffing now. "It's not my fault I had a brain fart."

I had a lot more to say, but my rant was cut short by a lot of rocking back and forth. They were trying to tip us, I think, or make us puke. One of the two. Probably the former. You never want to see someone lose their lunch in a brand-new car. I doubt that changes once you're dead.

We instinctively grabbed hold of one another. I didn't feel too weird doing it because he did it, too. I don't think either one of us knew how this was going to end. I know *I* didn't.

"What the heck are we going to do now?" I asked.

I tried to be as cool as a cucumber, but I was anything but. This was the first time throughout this whole experience that we didn't seem to have a way out. Will was thinking the same thing. I could tell from the look on his face.

"There is *no* chance I'm getting out of this car," he said. "Neither are you."

I chuckled.

"No argument here."

"Hey boys?" said an amplified voice. It completely threw us for a loop because it was clearly coming from out there. We tried looking for the source, but we couldn't see beyond the zombies.

"I'm afraid you need to come on out of that car. Fun's over, okay?"

Oh, okay, sir. Sure. We'll come right out. All you need to do is call off your zombies. The nerve of this guy, whoever he was. Needless to say, we didn't so much as entertain the idea of stepping from that car.

The guy gave a nervous sort of laugh. I still couldn't see his face, but I'm willing to bet he was sweating to beat the band. Sorry. That was another grandfather line.

"Um, boys, these gentlemen are liable to tip this car right over, if you don't come out," he continued. "And, I doubt anyone here wants to see *that*."

Suddenly, a crowd of people began chanting, *"Do it! Do it! Do it!"* I would have found it kind of funny, if I wasn't inside of it. I started to wonder just what the heck was going on out there. I mean, honestly, just when I thought things couldn't get any crazier, this guy shows up with an audience.

"Oh boy. Let's keep in mind, ladies and gentlemen, that if they destroy the car, neither one of them will win it," he reminded the crowd. "And, they've had their hands on it for a little over twenty hours now."

This announcement silenced the crowd for all of three seconds. Then, they broke into their chant all over again.

"Do it! Do it! Do it!"

Meanwhile, in the car, we were both sporting the shocked emoji face.

"What the heck is going on out there?" Will asked. He hadn't looked this perplexed since our last big Math test. "What's all this about having their hands on this car for twenty hours?"

"Beats me," I answered. "I know there used to be a game show where you could win a new truck or something like that if you were able to keep your hand on it for longer than the other contestants. My dad loved it for some reason. Last I checked, though, there weren't any zombies on the show."

"Yeah. Well, before today, there weren't any zombies period, except for in horror movies."

It was definitely a different world we lived in now, with different rules. And, it seemed like these things weren't going away anytime soon. I'd been avoiding eye contact with them as much as I could – purely out of fear. It was almost like they were each Medusa, and, if I so much as looked into their eyes, then I'd be turned to stone. I was pretty sure it couldn't turn me into stone, but it was certainly capable of leaving me frozen in fear. I knew I would eventually have to face my fears though. We all needed to. With that in mind, I decided the time was right to do just that. And, so I did. *I faced my fears* – from behind the pane of glass that was the back passenger side window.

There they were, the first two zombies to show up at that window.

Man! They were ugly. Their eyes weren't quite as soulless as some of the others, but they definitely looked like they had crawled right out of their graves. The sad part was their loved ones mustn't have cared too much about them because they weren't even wearing nice suits. And, one of them even had some serious five o'clock shadow going – or Dad's Saturday face. I only called it that because Dad always had the same look going on Saturdays.

"*Wait a minute!*" I shouted.

"*What?*" Will asked, after he'd just about fallen to the floor at my feet. It was too bad he didn't have his seatbelt on like me.

"*That one has five o'clock shadow!*" I said, pointing him out.

"Okay," he said, now staring intently at his face. "And?"

"And, how many zombies have you seen with five o'clock shadow?"

He only shrugged his shoulders. What I was getting at hadn't quite registered with him. To be fair, though, we were both pretty tired. Probably not as tired as somebody who had been touching a car for over twenty hours, but tired nonetheless.

"That's not a zombie," I explained. "That's a guy – a really tired, messy-looking guy. I mean, he probably smells like a zombie, but I'm pretty sure he isn't one."

Will opened his mouth to respond, but something about the other zombie caught his eye.

"*That one has an MP3 player!*" he said, all excited. "Look. You can even see the earphone dangling from his ear."

He was right. I would have bet any amount of money that those two weren't zombies. *Man!* Talk about a missed opportunity. We could have gotten out of this mess well before we were surrounded.

We both started looking from zombie to zombie, trying to figure out which ones were the real deal and which ones weren't. Sadly, the rest of them checked out. They were legit.

"*Ugh!*" Will groaned. "Why couldn't we have noticed this earlier? We could have been long gone by now."

He kept venting to me, but I ignored him. He was like a broken record. Listening to him was getting me nowhere, unless you counted further down in the dumps as somewhere.

Suddenly, I spied with my little eye a glimmer of hope. Okay. It was a door handle, but it was made of metal, and, if the light hit it just right, it did glimmer. Anyways, it gave me a new idea – well, more of an escape plan really. I looked up at the two guys, who were no longer zombies, to find them positioned just right for what I had in mind.

"*Hey!*" I finally interrupted him. "Look where those two dudes are standing. They're right in front of the door."

Will nodded, but then looked to me to continue. So, I did.

"I say we open that door, and make a break for it."

He nodded again, and then reached for the handle. Our escape wasn't as clean as I thought it would be. I could hear all sorts of shouting behind us. I think they had finally let go of the car, and I think we might have had a lot to do with it. Sorry, but all is fair in love, war, and fleeing from zombies.

"*ALLIE CAT'S!*" I shouted. "*That's* where we should go."

I hadn't been that excited to see the sign for Allie Cat's Restaurant since I was like five or six. It was one of those theme restaurants every parent should have loved. It kept us kids busy so we didn't act up, and it tuckered us out. It was a win-win for my parents. There was an arcade, a ginormous ball pit, and just about every character from *The Allie Cat Show* walking around, entertaining the kids. They had Allie Cat herself, Mangy Angie, and the rest of the crew. The best part was the plates were shaped like trash can lids. That way, kids – and, I guess some adults – got to eat like the characters from the show. You also had the option of drinking your milkshake from a saucer. Mom and Dad never let me do that though. They thought it was a little too much. Maybe they were right, but it still would have been kind of cool.

"Are you kidding me?" Will asked. "Absolutely not. That place is for little kids."

"But, that's the perfect..." I started to say.

"No," he said, cutting me off in a fashion that probably would have made both my mother and his mother proud.

He gave the entranceway a double take, and then all of a sudden had a change of heart.

"On second thought, maybe it isn't the worst idea in the world," he admitted.

Curious, I also gave the entranceway a closer look. All I found was Ricky the Rat handing out coupons for the restaurant. I always found it a little strange that they wanted an overgrown rat roaming around their restaurant, entertaining guests. However, they did need to stick with the back-alley theme, and I guess he was kind of cute – for a rat. I'll be honest though, his tail always bugged me.

"Are you thinking what I'm thinking?" he asked, beaming with pride.

"I hate to break it to you, but I spent the last of my allowance on those photos we left back in the booth," I explained. "So, even with a coupon, we're kind of out of luck. Besides …"

"Why don't we try this again?" he suggested. "Are you thinking what I'm thinking?"

He repeatedly pointed to Ricky and then back at us. I gave Ricky the Rat another look to see what else I could come up with. I figured I owed it to Will.

"Ah," I said, thinking I might have had it. "You want to ask Ricky the Rat for help, right?"

He looked so let down by my response. I honestly didn't get it. I mean, what on earth did he want to hear?

"What then?" I asked.

He let out a drawn-out sigh, and finally gave me the rundown. And, just so you know, I no longer felt like such a fool once he finished laying it all out.

"If we can get our hands on – or rather our body in – one of those costumes, then the zombies will more than likely have no idea where we are. Makes sense, right?"

I'm guessing I was probably the one who looked let down this time around. This plan wouldn't work for a number of reasons.

"What?" he asked, obviously taken aback by my reaction.

"Look at the size of those costumes," I said, motioning to Ricky.

"And, look at the size of us. You can't possibly think it would be a good fit. We're way too short."

He shook his head, grinning away. He was apparently in on something I wasn't privy to.

"We'll be fine," he assured me. "Either you'll sit on my shoulders or I'll sit on yours. Easy-peasy. They do it on TV all the time."

I slammed my palm into my forehead, with a little more force than I wanted to use. Chalk it up to adrenaline, I guess.

"Dude, we can barely stay on each other's shoulders for chicken fights in the pool," I reminded him. "And, that's before we even get into the actual fight. Trust me. This unfortunately has disaster written all over it. But we really don't have anything else up our sleeve, so..."

He suddenly had an ear-to-ear grin going.

"*That's the spirit!*" he shouted, raising his hand for a high five. "Now, up top."

I was hoping he meant I'd be on his shoulders. Wishful thinking, I guess.

I gave him a lazy sort of high-five. He was so excited I doubt he even noticed.

"And, don't worry," he said. "Since I'm stronger than you, I'll be on the bottom."

I was just about to debate that point when it dawned on me that I'd pretty much be arguing in favor of me being on the bottom. Oh, he was *good*. I almost fell for it.

"You're right," I conceded. "I'm a weakling when it comes right down to it."

He suddenly looked a little concerned.

"Oh, hey, I didn't say all of that," he replied. "You're strong. Just not in the..."

I shook my head, with what I hoped was a convincing enough pout.

"Look," he began. "You can be on the bottom. I don't need to be. I just figured the sturdier, the..."

"I couldn't agree more!" I quickly exclaimed. "I'll get over it. Don't worry. It isn't worth us getting caught over."

"You're sure?" he asked. I could tell he felt a little guilty.

"Yeah," I answered. "Don't worry. We're good."

He nodded, and then we headed into Allie Cat's.

Inside, we found what seemed like all of the characters from the show mingling about. *Dang it!* This wasn't good. After all, if they were all present and accounted for, then how were we supposed to get our hands on a costume?

"*Paulie Pigeon!*" Will shouted. "Where is he? Do you see him anywhere?"

Oh yeah! Paulie Pigeon! That's right! I'd almost forgotten about him, and he was a fan favorite. At least, he was always one of my favorites. He was especially fun if you were eating spaghetti because he'd come right over to your table, bury his beak in your spaghetti, and suck a piece right up into his mouth as though it were a worm. It was hysterical. Actually, now that I think about it, I guess it was pretty gross. I mean, we're talking about a complete stranger eating your food, without actually asking your permission. Who cares though? Fun is fun, right?

"*Perfect!*" I said.

"Right?" Will continued. "Now, we just need to figure out where they keep the costumes."

That should have been easy enough. All the doors were clearly marked. One of them had to read Employees Only or something along those lines. Even a Keep Out would have done the trick. Eventually, we found what we were looking for.

"Beware of Humans?" Will read aloud. "Do you think this is where they keep the costumes?"

"Maybe," I said, not altogether sure of it. "I mean, what else could be behind this door?"

"There's only one way to find out," he continued.

We checked the area to make sure we weren't being followed – by either the living or the dead. Everyone in there seemed to be too busy having a blast to even notice us. I tried the handle, and, much to my surprise, it wasn't locked. For some reason, I always figured the Employees Only door was locked. Thankfully, I was wrong.

To tell you the truth, I always thought the room "where the magic happened" would have been a lot cleaner and have fewer napkin dispensers. This looked more like a break room. Actually, it looked a lot like the teachers' lounge at school. I happened to walk by it once while they were all on lunch break, and my science teacher, Mr. Ross, just about blew a gasket when he saw me looking in. He acted like I was going to run and tell all of my friends, so we could crash the party.

Hanging on a hook back by the vending machine, I could see our disguise. It actually looked kind of sad, folded over, with no life in it.

"Aw, look at it," I said, getting perhaps a little too emotional. "He was my favorite character, and now he's just hanging back here, while everyone else is out having fun."

Will clearly wasn't as sentimental as me – not when it came to *Allie Cat* characters anyways.

"You know it's just a costume, right?" he cautiously asked. "Paulie Pigeon isn't real. You know that, right?"

"Obviously," I said, trying to save a little face. "It's just that *The Allie Cat Show* was a huge part of my childhood – specifically my Saturday mornings. And, when this place first opened, I tried to get my parents to bring us here like every weekend for months."

Will sighed. "Well, I mean, look at it this way," he began. "You're actually going to get to play your favorite character from the show. How cool is that? And what better way to honor him than by getting into that costume and being the best Paulie Pigeon you can be?"

My eyes instantly lit up, though he couldn't see them. He was saying everything I needed to hear to get me out of the funk I was in.

"You're right," I said. "Maybe I can even eat someone's spaghetti off their plate."

"*What?*" he asked, pretending to gag. At least, I hope he was only pretending. "That's…"

"What he does," I interrupted him.

He simply shook his head.

"Knock yourself out," he said. "Just don't overdo it, okay?"

"*Sick!*" I shouted, clapping my hands together.

"Exactly what I was thinking," I heard Will mutter just as I started to jog on over there.

I wasted no time in taking it down from its hook. Will took his sweet time getting over there. You'd have thought he was my father on Christmas Day.

We stared at one another for a moment, and then at the costume itself. It was pretty obvious neither of us knew how to approach this situation. Normally, when someone did it on TV or in a movie, the director would show the two people coming up with the plan and then he'd cut right to them already in the costume. We really could have used a scene showing exactly how they got in there and how they got up onto one another's shoulders. Come to think of it, such a scene never even made its way into the deleted scenes. How on earth were we supposed to know then?

A chair. That was how they did it. Or, at least, that was how *we* did it. I hopped onto one of the chairs, Will stood right in front of me with Paulie's legs already on, I climbed onto his shoulders just like we would for a chicken fight in the pool, and I carefully pulled the top half of the costume on. And, just like that, Paulie Pigeon was born...or rather reborn.

We were a little wobbly at first, which made me all the more nervous since we didn't have a pool of water to fall into this time around. If we fell now, chances were pretty good we'd be hitting the floor hard. Needless to say, I wasn't too gung-ho anymore over the idea of bending over somebody's plate to help myself to their spaghetti for a few cheap laughs. As unsteady as we were, I was liable to face-plant onto their table, and I had zero interest in making it to anyone's epic fail compilation. Thanks, but no thanks.

"I'm thinking we should probably practice a little in here before we head out there," I suggested. "What do you think?"

"Not the worst idea in the world," Will's muffled voice replied, as he fought to steady himself.

I'll be honest with you. I was starting to think that maybe this wouldn't work out so hot for us. Let's just say the plan – like most plans, I guess – ran a lot smoother in my mind.

We navigated around that room very slowly for the first few minutes – even slower than the times when I would carry a big tray of food to my table at lunch. The only difference being that I was trying not to spill my food in front of an entire school then, whereas now I was trying to keep myself from cracking my head open on the concrete floor. To be honest with you, I could have stayed in that back room for hours until we got it right, but Will had something else in mind.

"Okay," he said. "We need to get out there, or else someone will find us back here and probably kick us out of the restaurant. If that happens, we'll be back to square one."

He was right. It definitely wasn't in our best interest to hole up back there.

I took a deep breath, and then pointed to the door in dramatic fashion. Of course, he couldn't see me, so I needed to give him the green light another way.

"Giddyup," I said, giving him a little kick to the side.

"I will drop you right now, if you try that again," he quickly informed me. "I promise."

"I'm sorry," I apologized, reaching down to pat his side. It took just about everything I had in me not to burst into laughter. "It won't happen again, okay? I swear."

"It had better not," he replied.

"It won't. And, before we start for real, can you see at all? Or, am I completely going to be our eyes?"

"Well, I suppose I could pull the fabric aside and see from down here," he said, which made me feel a little more relaxed for the time being. "But that could cause a couple of problems. First and foremost, it could totally give us away. Secondly, it could ruin the experience for any little kids out there, and I'd rather *not* be the one who does that."

He had unfortunately raised two great points. I guess I had to man up and do my job.

"You'll be fine," he assured me. "Just keep your directions simple. That's all. You know, right, left, and straight. That sort of thing. Don't toss out any of that nine o'clock or two o'clock nonsense, though, because it'll only mess me up."

"Okay," I agreed. "And, now, what about the number of steps you'll need to take? Should I just shout the numbers out?"

He paused for a moment. He must have been mulling that one over.

"Nah," he finally said. "You'd better not. After all, I have bigger feet than you and longer strides. The simpler, the better. Right, left, straight, stop, and go. We'll leave it at that."

I opened the door as soon as we got over there. I always have this feeling somebody's going to open the door right into me. I don't know why. I mean, it's only happened to me once, and it wasn't a big deal. I'd gotten out of the way in time. If it happened this time around, though, I wasn't so sure we'd be able to sidestep it. That's why I didn't want to take any chances.

"*Wow!*" he exclaimed. "We're already out here, huh?"

I quickly shushed him. "*Dude!* My belly shouldn't be talking."

I could feel him suddenly tense up. Then, he halted, which nearly sent me into a nosedive.

"*Dude!*" I barked, again. "You need to tell me when you're going to do that. I almost fell."

He didn't respond. Either he was mad at me for snapping at him – twice no less – or he was keeping quiet so as not to give us away. It easily could have been for either reason, but I convinced myself it was the latter. In the event he *was* giving me the silent treatment, however, I figured it was best to just give him my directions.

"Okay," I said. "Go forward…now right. *Whoa!* Slow down. There's a table right in front of us."

I came dangerously close to giving him another little kick to the side. I'm glad I caught myself. And, I know I still sounded a little bossy, but it was nearly impossible to do this without sounding bossy.

"Sorry," I apologized. "It's just that…"

I could feel our right leg (well, his) moving up and down in quick bursts. He must have been tapping his foot in frustration. I didn't

CHAPTER 13 | 91

waste any more time trying to be polite. Instead, I just set about guiding him around the restaurant.

I started to get a little clever with how I worded my directions. For instance, instead of simply telling him to stop whenever some kid wanted to take a picture with me, I'd say something along the lines of *"Sure. I'd love to take a picture with you."* Will stopped walking every time he heard this. I must say we had a pretty good system.

It was working out just fine until some new diners showed up. They weren't there for pizza though. They were there for us. They were zombies.

"We have company," I said, trying my best to remain calm.

I was a little panicky. This was the first time I needed to rely on someone else's speed to get me out of a jam. I'm just glad it was Will I was counting on. He was quicker than me anyways.

"Just remain calm," Will said. At least, I think that was what he said. He was evidently trying to be as quiet as a church mouse about it. Quiet as a church mouse? I never quite understood how that one got so popular. I'd never even seen one mouse at church, let alone enough of them for that saying to be as common as it was.

"I'm trying," I said. "Believe me, I am trying."

"They can't see us if we're under here," he continued. "Just remember that, and you should be fine."

This was easy for him to say. I think he was so calm because he didn't have to look at them. I tried following his advice. It didn't seem to be working though. Even though they couldn't have possibly seen me, they kept getting closer and closer. Eventually, they were right up in my face, checking me out. Maybe they smelled me. That was the only reason I could think of. I gave my armpit a whiff. Nothing. That is to say it didn't smell any worse than usual.

"Back up," I blurted out. I was hoping *they* would back up, but I mistakenly said it out loud, so Will must have thought I was talking to him.

"Okay," he said, and then took a few steps backwards.

"Wait!" I shouted. "Where are we going?"

"Uh-oh!" he shouted.

He quickly stopped, but my momentum kept me leaning backwards, which caused him to reel backwards. I hated this feeling. There was nothing I could do to slow us down. Absolutely nothing. In fact, it took everything I had just to maintain balance.

As it turned out, I didn't have to maintain balance for too long. He backed us right up into the ball pit. Well, I should say he sent *me* flying into the ball pit. He, on the other hand, stayed put once we slammed into it.

I'm not sure which one of us had it worse. I was practically upside down in a ball pit, while he was left standing out there with his face exposed. They could see him now. I, at least, still had the Paulie Pigeon head on. Of course, it probably wouldn't make maneuvering around in that ball pit any easier. I considered taking it off, but was too afraid.

"*Hey, everyone!*" some kid shouted. "*Check it out! Paulie Pigeon's in here with us!*"

This had disaster written all over it.

I was about to shush the kid, but then I just decided to go along with it. I figured just maybe it would work in my favor to have a bunch of kids crowd around me. I was still worried about Will, but there wasn't a heck of a lot I could do for him from in there. I decided to do what I imagined Paulie Pigeon himself would do if he ever found himself inside of a ball pit with an audience. I treated it like a bird bath. I swam around for a little while and even pretended to give myself a bath. The kids loved it. They were really eating it up. Unfortunately, I couldn't say the same for Allie Cat, who I failed to notice was standing right outside of the pit.

"*Hey!*" she shouted. "*We're not supposed to go into the ball pit!*"

We stopped what we were doing and gave her our full attention.

"How come?" I asked. "We're having fun. Isn't that what it's all about?"

"*Yeah!*" some kid agreed. "Don't you *want* us to have fun?"

Allie looked around at every last kid in the pit. All eyes were on her.

"Whatever," she said. "It's your funeral."

She then stormed off to a chorus of boos courtesy of the kids –
and me. She asked for it. Personally, I think she just didn't like being
upstaged. If it makes you feel any better, she did turn and literally hiss
at us. We were all taken aback by it at first. After all, it isn't easy seeing
the nasty side of a beloved character. We celebrated our victory soon
after though.

Unfortunately, our celebration was short-lived. Allie returned, and
she wasn't alone. She had some stuffy-looking guy I'm guessing was
my manager with her. He didn't say a word. All he did was direct me
out of there with his thumb. He was acting like a real big shot.

Another, even louder chorus of boos erupted. The kids were really
causing a scene. Is it bad that I was proud of them? I looked around.
Even the zombies seemed a little distracted by it. I figured now was
our chance to get out of there – meaning mine and Will's.

Out of nowhere, the kids all rushed the side of the pit. I could tell
both Allie and the manager didn't know what to make of this unexpected turn of events. I quickly devised a brilliant plan to get out of
the pit unnoticed. I joined the kids, pretty much getting right in the
center of them, and then sort of ducked out from under Paulie's head,
leaving it resting there on the surface amongst the kids. No one would
be the wiser. Like I said, it was brilliant. The next step in the plan was
to sneak over to the entrance to the pit and climb out. It worked like a
charm. In fact, when I looked back, I could still see the manager
getting on my case. He had no idea he was yelling at a costume. I don't
think the kids did either.

Luckily, the zombies were still distracted for the most part. This
bought me just enough time to get Will and get out of there. He was
still a little shaken up from when he slammed into the pit, but he soon
snapped out of it.

"Are you ready to get out of here?" I asked. "Or, do you need a
minute?"

"I don't think we have a minute," he said, motioning to a few
zombies who didn't seem as distracted as the others. "Let's get out of
here."

He didn't even bother to take his pigeon legs off. He just started booking it for the door. I was way ahead of him for once. Granted, I *was* running on human legs, so I did have something of an advantage. At one point, I glanced back to find him sitting on the floor, pulling the pigeon legs off. I would have been worried about this, if all of the commotion at the ball pit wasn't still going on.

The good thing is he got them off in a flash. Easy to get on and easy to get off. I'm glad pigeon costumes weren't like snow suits. Otherwise, we'd have probably been zombie food.

Believe it or not, we headed out into the mall just as a couple of zombies were headed into Allie Cat's. Sorry, fellas, but it looks like you were a little too late to the party. Lucky for us.

14

"I REALLY WISH we didn't throw our zombie costumes away," Will said as we hurried through the mall en route to the nearest exit.

"Why?" I asked. "If anything, they probably would have slowed us down."

"Maybe," he said. "Then again, we might have been able to blend right in with them."

Wow! He might have been on to something. It's just too bad we hadn't thought of that earlier, back in the theater. Granted, we really didn't know we had a bunch of *actual* zombies on our hands. We thought we just had a bunch of jokers in costumes messing with us.

"Oh well," I grumbled. "There's no point in crying over spilled milk."

Suddenly, Will stopped walking. Instinctively, I scanned the area to see if we had undead company. I couldn't find any – not anywhere near us anyways.

"What's going on?" I asked. "Why'd you stop?"

"I agree that there's no use in crying over spilled milk," he said. "But what if we were to get some new milk?"

I had no idea where he was headed with this nonsense. To be

honest, I was afraid he'd lost it. I was afraid all this craziness had finally taken its toll on the poor kid.

"You'll be alright," I explained, gently patting him on the shoulder before trying to usher him along.

"No," he said, brushing me off. "Look."

He pointed a few stores down to Halloween Bazaar. It was one of those Halloween stores that sold just about everything you could think of that was supposed to scare you out of your wits. They're only in the mall like once a year from September through November. I quickly understood what he was getting at. It was actually kind of brilliant. Normally, I wasn't a huge fan of this store. Some of the masks gave me the willies in years past. Well, that and their costumes tended to cost an arm and a leg most of the time. However, I guess if getting my hands on one was possibly going to save me an arm and a leg this time around, then it'd be worth it.

"Let's do it," I said, fully on board.

He was psyched that I recognized his genius for once.

The place was mobbed, which I guess made sense since Halloween was just around the corner. And, as I'm sure you can guess by now, the must have costume at the time was that of the zombie. Essentially, we were right back where we started. Only, this time around, we needed to figure out who was *dressed* like a zombie and who was the real thing. You see, back in the theater, before we knew any better, we figured everyone was dressed up for the occasion.

"Oh great," Will said, with a sigh. "Why do costumes have to look so real nowadays?"

"I know," I replied. "As if this isn't stressful enough already."

"Well, we need to do this no matter what," he explained. "So, we might as well get to it."

I nodded in agreement and we entered the store through the fake, Styrofoam columns with the fake, Styrofoam gargoyles sitting atop them, and then made our way past row after row of Halloween-themed paper cups, plates, napkins, and streamers. I don't know why there were so many Halloween party supplies. Then again, I wasn't invited to too many of them. It always seemed like something the older kids did once they outgrew trick-or-treating.

"I think we should just go right to the costumes," Will continued. "We need to treat this like a bank robbery. Just get in and get out."

I rolled my eyes. Honestly, he shouldn't have expected any less.

"You watch too many movies," I pointed out.

"Maybe," he reluctantly agreed. "We still can't afford to waste any time in here though."

"Agreed," I said. "So, it'll save us time if we find a zombie costume that's already together. If we need to put it together as we go, it'll obviously take longer. Oh, and make sure it fits, too."

He shook his head, clearly flustered. "Okay," he said. "This is taking way too long. Let's just get our costumes on before we end up somebody's lunch."

It didn't take us long to find our zombie costumes. Surprisingly, it did take us long to find our size, even in the children's costume aisle. I mean, for crying out loud, they even had zombie costumes for the youngsters. I'm talking four and five-year-olds. Even *I* wouldn't have put a five-year-old in a zombie costume. They were only a couple of years out of being teddy bears and ladybugs. That's a pretty quick jump to the undead, if you ask me. *Sheesh!*

"I've got mine," Will announced, and apparently held it up immediately.

"So do I," I said, pulling mine down from its hook.

I turned to discover we were holding the same exact costume. Any other time, this would have resulted in a round of rock-paper-scissors, but it didn't really matter to me anymore. Will, on the other hand, was clearly agitated.

"*You always do this!*"

"This isn't about who has the better costume," I explained. "It's about survival, dude."

"Yeah, you're right," he admitted. "Sorry. I forgot we were..."

He didn't finish his thought. Not because I cut him off though. I believe he pretty much cut himself off before he said something he figured would sound utterly ridiculous. I guess, I couldn't really blame him. I mean, we *were* kids. Yeah, you have to grow up fairly quickly when something like this happens, but not every part of you is going to grow up. It just isn't realistic. I don't care who you are.

"Hey, should we get some fake blood and smear that on us, too?" he asked.

I looked to see if there was any nearby because it wasn't the worst idea in the world, but it wasn't absolutely necessary, so we were good either way. Well, we weren't *good* exactly. What I meant to say was it probably wouldn't have helped or hurt our chances of getting out of this alive.

"I don't see any," I answered. "We should be fine though. Let's just get these on and get out of here."

"Right," he agreed. "One question. How much are they?"

It never even occurred to me to check the price. In fact, I didn't even scope out where the cash registers were. To be completely honest with you, my plan was for us to get them on and get out of there. He must have seen it on my face. I went slack-jawed.

"You weren't planning on paying for these, were you?" he asked, sporting a smirk. He had me. Dang it.

"No," I answered, rolling my eyes.

"Well, well, well," he continued, grinning to beat the band now. "So, it's not okay when I want to shoplift, but it's perfectly fine when you want to? Is that what you're saying?"

"We're talking apples and oranges here," I replied. "We *need* these. It's not even close to the same thing, when you really think about it. I mean, if anything, you lugging around a huge bag of toys would have slowed us down. This, on the other hand, is going to help us out big time. So there."

See what I mean? There's more of that inability to grow up in every single way. Apparently, I was as guilty as the next kid when it came to this – the next kid being Will, of course. Once I recovered from this reality slap, I found him still grinning away like he'd pulled just about the greatest practical joke in history on me.

"Just get your costume on. Okay, wise guy?"

He nodded, still beaming a little. Very rarely did he get the win when it came to our battle of wits, so I let him revel in his moment. Actually, it probably wasn't even a full moment before he was pulling his costume from its bag. I followed suit. Nobody even seemed to notice. It's probably because they were all trying on masks left and right. Why, I don't know. What I do know is every time I've ever slipped one of them on, I swear I could feel the sweat and maybe even snot of every person who had pulled that sucker on before me. Gross, right? This was the only time it came in handy having those glasses stuck to my head. It meant I wouldn't be tempted to try on a sweaty, snot-filled mask.

I'll be honest with you. I mistakenly grabbed the wrong size, and just went with it. It was as tight as all get out on me, and I wasn't even that big for my age. If anything, you could probably say I was on the smaller side. Just to see how far off I was, I checked the label. It turned out my costume was stitched together for a seven to eight-year-old. The pants didn't even come close to touching my sneakers.

"Where's the flood?" Will jokingly asked.

"Shut up," I said, but grinned regardless. Honestly, I would have probably asked him the same thing.

"You're never gonna be able to run in those, you know," he pointed out. "You're gonna be way too stiff. Maybe you should..."

"Good," I interrupted, which may have come across as childish. "Zombies don't run anyways. I'll be more convincing this way. In fact, I was thinking you should do the same," I said, just to sound a little more full of it.

"Nope," he quickly replied, "I'm good."

"Whatever. Suit yourself."

Much like misery, uncomfortableness and embarrassment also love company. Makes sense, I guess. We pulled our masks on in unison like we were about to rob a bank. Yikes. Maybe he wasn't the only one who had seen too many movies. Eh, chalk it up to being a couple of ten-year-olds.

As secretly as we could, we made for the exit. Was there a tiny pang of guilt slowing me down? Perhaps. However, I just blamed it on the tight pants, and continued on my way.

We weren't even to the party supplies yet when we learned our costume ploy was an epic failure. The zombies were suddenly upon us, and it was clear they knew we weren't with them. They were all over us. I could have sworn I felt one grab my mask. This was enough for me. I gave him what he wanted. I pulled it right off and tossed it at him. Will no longer had his on either.

"So much for that plan," he shouted. *"Come on!"*

He quickly grabbed hold of my arm and dragged me off towards the grown-ups' costume aisle. It was mobbed back there – more so than in the children's aisle.

"We'll be better off back there," he insisted, "I'm sure of it."

Before we entered the aisle and hopefully into hiding if even for a little while, I peeled the remainder of my costume off. I felt like a new man once I got out of that thing. Even though his couldn't have been nearly as constricting as mine, Will stripped down, too. The way I saw it, if we weren't fooling any of the zombies, then it was pointless to leave them on anyways. And, this way, we had no reason to feel guilty.

"I bet you're glad to have that thing off," he said.

"I am," I said. "And, when this is all over with, I'll finally be able to really breathe, again."

He shook his head as if I'd been making a mountain out of a mole hill. Now, I wouldn't say he was enjoying all of this by any stretch, but he definitely didn't seem to be taking it as seriously as I was. If anything, I was making a mountain range out of a mountain, but, if you ask me, I wasn't even guilty of that. After all, this was an unheard-of type of craziness we were experiencing – the likes of which nobody had seen before – least of all a couple of ten-year-olds.

"You know, you could stand to take this a little more seriously," I suggested.

"Me?" he asked, flabbergasted. *"I'm* the one who's had all of the good ideas so far. I mean, *this* was a good one until they figured us out. All you've done was squirt a bunch of bubbles at them. Whoop-dee-doo."

Was he serious? I wondered. Had he suddenly gone delusional?

"The costumes were *your* idea?" I asked. "Seriously?"

He stared at me in disbelief for a moment.

"Yeah," he answered, matter-of-factly.

Come to think of it, they *were* his idea. It was just too bad I couldn't back track by that point or else I would have looked even more foolish.

"Yeah, well, it was a stupid idea anyways. I'm glad *I* didn't come up with it."

Suddenly, without any kind of a warning, he gave me a pretty good shove. I'll be honest, it sent me reeling back a few steps. In fact, I'm surprised I was able to keep my balance at all. That's how good of a shove it was.

"Oh, really?" I shouted. "You want to do *this*?"

"*Yeah!*" he shouted, nodding.

My jaw dropped a little further than it already had. Chalk it up to the salt he had just added to my already wounded ego, I suppose.

Unfortunately, there was only one way for any normal ten-year-old boy to respond. Well, it was the only way *I* could think of anyways. In hindsight, I sort of wish I had more self-control and less strength at that moment. I rushed at him, and shoved him right to the floor. I suddenly felt every eye in that aisle on me.

I immediately felt horrible. Yeah, he shoved me first, but he didn't give it everything he had. I pretty much did. I felt even worse when I noticed the look on his face. He was frightened – practically terrified by the looks of it. He even started pointing at me; well, near me anyways.

"Dude, relax," I said, a little surprised I had to. "I doubt anything's broken."

I gave him a sort of once-over to see if perhaps I was missing something. Perhaps he'd landed wrong. In the meantime, I noticed he was still pointing to the same spot even though I wasn't standing there any longer.

"What's going on?" I asked, slowly turning to see for myself.

I wish I hadn't taken my time checking it out because it almost cost me a lot more than just time. It turned out I had a zombie right behind me. I must have been too caught up in mixing it up with Will to notice.

"*Argh!*" I shouted, stumbling backwards towards Will. I ended up taking a seat on the floor beside him.

The zombie was closing in on us and there was literally nothing we could do – nor was there anywhere for us to go.

"*You know what?*" Will shouted. "*I'm sick of this!*"

He jumped to his feet and rushed the zombie.

"*No!*" I shouted. "*What are you doing?*"

Before I could muster enough courage to help him, he gut-punched the zombie. It let out an unexpected, human-like groan.

"*What the heck is wrong with you, kid?*" we heard someone close by ask.

Within seconds, the zombie pulled his mask off and revealed himself to be just another dopey guy acting like an overgrown kid in a candy store.

Sheesh! Talk about a convincing mask. I honestly couldn't tell the difference between him and the real thing. Before I knew what had happened, I was getting yet another look at the real thing. A handful of them had surrounded me. It was bad. It had gotten to the point where I couldn't even see Will anymore – or anyone else for that matter.

"*Will?*" I shouted. "*You still there?*"

I didn't hear from him at first. Naturally, I started panicking.

"*Will?*" I shouted, once again. This was by far the most scared I'd been since this whole thing began. It didn't help matters that I was still seated on the floor. I considered reaching up and trying my luck pulling one or two of their masks off, but I chickened out at the last second. I didn't want to risk being bitten in case I was wrong. The last thing I wanted was to be turned into a zombie myself.

Suddenly, it dawned on me why I might not have been hearing back from Will. I feared the worst; the worst being that *he* might have been turned into one. A few questions I didn't want to ask myself swept through my mind. First of all, how was I going to make it on my own? Not just out of this mess, but through life in general. Then, was he going to bite me? And, finally, what was I going to tell his mom?

I really didn't have much of a plan going forth without him. Hopelessly sitting there, waiting to be devoured, didn't exactly get the old creative juices flowing. I'll be honest, it seemed as though I was destined to join him. I know it's pathetic, but the best I could come up with at that point was to simply close my eyes and hope they'd make short work of me – the shorter the better.

Within seconds, I felt one of them grab me under the armpits and hoist me to my feet. As startled as I was by this turn of events, I still kept my eyes shut, refusing to bear witness to my own demise. That might have been a little too much to stomach. Before long, I felt myself being shoved quite a ways and then suddenly left alone. When I had finally built up enough courage to open one of my eyes, I discovered that Will and I were back out in the mall – seemingly unharmed.

"The manager kicked us out," he informed me.

15

"Now, what?" I asked. "Do you have any other good ideas?"

I'm pretty sure he shot me an angry glare, with some frustration mixed in. At first, I didn't get why he was so upset with me. I mean, all I had done was ask him a simple question. Then, it occurred to me that he probably figured I was cracking wise.

"Oh, no," I added. "I didn't mean anything by it. I was honestly hoping you had a few more ideas up your sleeve. Sure, this one didn't work out so well for us, but that doesn't mean it was such a bad idea. Even the best ideas don't always work out the way you want them to, especially in crazy situations like this."

"Thanks," he said, finally dropping his tough guy demeanor. "I don't know. I wish I had more ideas. I think I'm all tapped out though."

Dang it! I was afraid of that. Now, I sort of felt bad. After all, I doubt it helped matters any that I was putting even more pressure on him. I was just trying to extend an olive branch to make up for the fight we had earlier – if you could even call it that. Truth be told, we probably would have been made fun of by all of the other boys at school for it. I mean, there were no punches thrown or anything. It was all shove, and there was no love for the shove in our bloodthirsty schoolyard.

"I just wish we could find a spot we'd be safe in for more than a couple of minutes at a time," he admitted.

"I know," I sullenly agreed. "This sucks. I mean, there doesn't seem to be *anywhere* for us to…"

This was when I first noticed them in there. Not the zombies, mind you. I'm talking about the dogs in the pet store. They were safe, just lying there behind the glass. As far as *I* could tell, they were safe anyways. It looked to me like nobody was getting in there with them without a set of keys. That ruled out zombies. Now, we just needed to get our hands on those keys.

"We need to get in there with those dogs," I said. "Then, we'll be safe."

He looked at me like I'd finally lost my mind.

"Okay," he calmly replied, arching his eyebrows before looking elsewhere. "Just in case, why don't I come up with something as well? How does that sound?"

He slowly shifted his focus back to me. I couldn't control myself. I began laughing, and it sort of turned into what I'm sure could have been confused with a cackle. This mustn't have helped my case any come to think of it.

"Look," I began, rolling my eyes. "I haven't lost my mind, if that's what you're thinking. I mean, think about it. *Zombies* can't get in there. They'd need a key, and they're obviously not going to go looking for one. We will, though, and we can just chill in there until this is all over."

Even though I did a pretty decent job explaining myself and proving to him I was still sane, it was clear he still had some concerns. Then again, who could really blame him? I'm sure it still seemed a little out there.

"Who knows how long that'll be though?" he asked. "I mean, I don't want to *starve* to death in there."

"We won't," I said, matter-of-factly. "I mean, they must have dog biscuits. Right?"

He was back to sizing me up for a straight-jacket, I think. "Never in a million years did I think I'd find myself eating dog biscuits without losing a bet," he pointed out.

"Me neither. But, then again, I never thought I'd be hightailing it around the mall, trying to get away from a bunch of zombies either."

He shrugged. "Good point," he admitted.

As luck would have it, we entered the store to find a dog-training class in session. I figured this would probably work in our favor. I obviously didn't know for sure, but I had a theory that dogs didn't take too well to zombies. I mean, they rarely appreciated me, and I was a living, breathing, and often times loveable (depending upon who you asked) human being who fed them – not fed on them. Anyways, if anything, I assumed the dogs would react to them in such a way that it was bound to cause enough of a commotion for us to snag the keys we needed to get to safety without anyone noticing.

I glanced back into the mall, hoping at least a few of them had seen us enter the store.

"What?" Will asked. "Did you leave something out there?"

"Yeah," I answered. "The zombies."

His jaw dropped. I was sure nothing coming out of my mouth that afternoon had initially made any sense to him. Like I alluded to though, none of this was old hat to us – or anybody else for that matter. Therefore, our conversations *should* have been filled with jaw-droppers and eye-buggers.

"Maybe I'm crazy," he said. "But it looks like you actually *want* them to follow us in here. Please tell me I'm wrong."

I grinned, which only confirmed his biggest fear.

"Okay," he cautiously continued. "Now, tell me there's, at least, a method to your madness, because I've gotta tell you…this is a little cray-cray even for you. No offense."

All I could do at that point was laugh, which I think might've rubbed him the wrong way – understandably so.

"I'm sort of banking on these dogs going into attack mode once they see a group of zombies enter the store," I explained. "Then, while everyone is distracted, we'll just slide behind the cash register stand

and try to find the keys to the dog room. It should work. Don't you think?"

"As well as any other plan, I guess," he admitted.

This one didn't seem quite as clever as the costume plan, but I'd say it was a close second. I was earning my keep. Plus, the costume plan wasn't all that successful when you really think about it. In fact, when it came right down to it, the zombies weren't really fooled at all.

I gave the area a quick once-over, mostly shifting my focus between the register stand and the dog room. Will, in the meantime, couldn't take his eyes off the entrance.

"Don't worry," I said. "They'll be here soon enough."

"Who's worried?" he asked.

I couldn't really tell whether or not he'd just made a funny. I'm sure deep down he was worried this wasn't going to end well for us.

Within moments, the first couple of them had entered the store. *Dang!* They hadn't given me nearly enough time to pinpoint the location of the key.

"I don't think the dogs have noticed them yet," Will said. "Maybe we should do something about this."

"Okay," I said. "And just what did you have in mind? Did you want me to run right over to them and greet them with open arms?"

"No," he replied, barely able to keep a straight face. "Maybe we can just start yelling or whistling or something along those lines. I don't know. All we need to do is get the dogs to look up just as the zombies are making their way through the store. It shouldn't be that hard."

I didn't really want to throw all of the other shoppers into the type of frenzy that might result in both them and some of the animals being trampled underfoot, so I went mining for my next great idea – and, man, was it an impressive one.

"*A dog whistle!*" I couldn't help but blurt out.

"Huh?" Will asked, turning to me. "Where?"

Where we stood, we weren't anywhere near where they kept the dog whistles, but I left him looking anyways. I couldn't resist.

"Anyways," he continued, looking as confused as ever. "Why do we need a dog whistle of all things? Why can't we just scream at the zombies? It's quicker that way, and we won't need to struggle with any packages, if you know what I mean."

He just had to add that jab in there, didn't he? Maybe it was a quick, little payback. It's funny, but I always thought revenge – even harmless ribbing – was a dish best served *cold*. Guess I was wrong, or whoever came up with that saying might have been wrong. I don't know.

I ignored it and offered up my explanation. "Because that might cause a commotion."

"Um, zombies have taken over the mall," he reminded me. "And, surprisingly enough, no one seems to mind."

I rolled my eyes. He mustn't have figured out what was going on yet. Luckily, I had.

"Look, everyone knows *Zombies: Too Close for Comfort* just came out," I said. "They also know it's the *biggest* movie out right now, so they probably think these are all just people in costumes. I mean, *we* did, so…"

He sighed – probably because I'd made plenty of sense. I was sort of wise beyond my years, but I guess I didn't have to look too far past the dog whistle plan to realize this.

"Yeah, but we're just a couple of kids," he pointed out. "They're supposed to be much smarter than us."

"Ahem," I interjected. "Speak for yourself, dude. This dog whistle idea was definitely something to write home about. In fact, I'd say this whole pet store idea was pretty impressive."

He shook his head. He was being a royal pain in the neck now.

"Fine," he said. "Whatever. Let's just find the stupid whistle and get this over with."

"Yes," I politely agreed, just to get him going – or rather keep him going.

I sauntered over to the dog toys section, beaming the whole way. If he'd seen my face, then he probably would have given me a dead arm or maybe even a Charley horse – and I probably would have deserved it.

Let the record show that I was a complete tool for taking my time getting over there. In fact, it put us right in harm's way. One of the larger zombies met me just shy of the milk bones and pig ears. I tossed a pig ear to him, hoping this would buy us some time. He didn't fall for it though. He just let it land on the floor behind him. Just beyond where it landed, I could see what I was there for. There were a couple of different dog whistles hanging side by side. They only looked marginally different, so I didn't have to think too long on this. After all, I wasn't there to compare product. I was there to save us from the undead, and getting my hands on one of those whistles was the first step.

"*You're getting too close to him!*" Will shouted, from somewhere behind me. "We'll have to go with Plan B."

What? Plan B? First of all, there was no Plan B. Secondly, I'd come much too far to give up so quickly on Plan A. This was *my* baby. If *he* wanted to abort the mission, that was fine for him. I was going to see this sucker through though.

"*I'm* not giving up," I said, turning to face him. "So..."

Unfortunately, I couldn't face him. Somehow, one of the zombies had gotten between us. I wasn't sure how. That is to say I wasn't entirely sure how he'd gotten past Will without sinking his teeth into him. Not that I wanted him to attack Will. I was just wondering what he had against me specifically. I guess I must have looked a little more appetizing than Will.

"What the heck?" I shouted. "Why are they only going after me this time?"

"What do you mean?" Will shouted back, sounding genuinely confused.

I didn't have time to respond to this for the simple reason that I was on the verge of being sandwiched in between two zombies. Neither of them looked to be letting up anytime soon. I quickly started weighing my options, which included trying to gauge who the slower of the zombies probably was and then, of course, who the smaller was. Either way, I think I was kidding myself if I thought I'd be able to force my way past either one of them.

Just as I was about to close my eyes and chalk this one up as my final loss – which also I might add included preparing myself for life as a zombie, a pack of dogs of several different breeds rushed at us from the training center. Off in the distance, I could see them spilling out through the gate, and, in some cases, even leaping over the fence. I'm telling you I was never so happy to see so many dogs running at me.

I couldn't wait to see what they were going to do to the zombies. Not that I was necessarily bloodthirsty or anything. It's just that these guys were chasing us all over that mall all afternoon, scaring the heck out of me at every turn. Not once did they let up. I just hoped the dogs weren't hurrying over there just to sniff and lick their hands or any of that nonsense. Sometimes, that's all a dog's after.

You're not going to believe it, but those little good-for-nothings made their way right around the zombies and surrounded Will instead. *Dang it!* I couldn't believe it. I'd lost all sorts of respect. What a horrible turn of events. Needless to say, this wasn't part of the plan at all. In fact, I hadn't even considered it a possibility.

"This doesn't make any sense!" Will shouted, with his back now up against the sales rack and the whistle lifted high above his head. "They were supposed to…"

He was quickly drowned out by the sound of dogs barking. Just about every one of them was focused on him. As if the zombies weren't enough, the poor kid now had this to deal with. Only one of them couldn't be bothered with him, and that's because it was busy gnawing away at a pig ear. This suddenly gave me my next great idea, which, unlike the last one, was sure to work. I was convinced of it.

I quickly grabbed a handful of pig ears from the bin and launched them into the air. They landed right in between Will and the dogs, and, within seconds, it was as though they no longer knew he was even there. It worked like a charm. Good for me.

"Good idea, man!" Will shouted, with a big grin on his face. *"Thank you, thank you, thank you!"*

As nice as it was to receive immediate praise – especially so quickly and with such passion – I knew we were nowhere near in the clear yet. We needed to get our hands on those keys ASAP.

"You can thank me later," I suggested, even though he already had thanked me – three times. "Just get to those keys. I'll try to keep them distracted in the meantime."

This shouldn't have been too difficult a task since they seemed to be ignoring Will anyways.

It was nice to have the dogs out of the picture for the time being, but, unfortunately, the zombies were still right there, looking as determined as ever to make a quick snack of me. I hadn't felt this helpless since the time I got into my one and thankfully only fight at school. I say thankfully because I've never been much of a fighter, and, before you call me out on it, I wasn't much of a lover either – not unless you call one slow dance with a girl at a birthday party a love life.

With this in mind, I did just what I did during my fight. I started flailing my arms like a madman, hoping one of them would connect for a punch. And, just like that time at school, I only successfully assaulted the air in front of me. How pathetic was it that even someone who'd been dead for who knows how long was able to dodge my punches? Embarrassing.

Fortunately, *some* good had come out of this horrendous display of fighting. In all the melee, if you could even call it that, Will had tracked down the key we needed. As luck would have it, the key was one less thing we needed to waste valuable time on. And, make no mistake, *all* of our time was valuable by that point.

He somehow had to get through all of us to even use the key. Easy enough. I motioned for him to just barrel his way right through them from the rear. They'd never see it coming.

I could see he was a little hesitant at first, and who could blame him? Only a maniac would charge at a group of zombies. Once I showed him there was really no other way to get to the promised land, though, he took a deep breath and got on with it. He put his head down and ran. I just hoped he wouldn't trip. Not only would he have probably been embarrassed, but our plan would have failed miserably. One more setback might have spelled disaster for us.

I'm not going to lie. Mixed in with my concern over whether or not he could maintain his balance was an undeniable sense of admiration. I mean, he was going for it. It was a gutsy move through and through. And, amazingly, he was through them within seconds. He grabbed hold of my arm on his way by and used just enough force to spin me right around so we were now both facing the door to the dog room.

"*That was awesome!*" I couldn't help but shout. "*Atta boy, Will!*"

"We're not out of this yet," he explained, as he desperately tried to unlock the door.

There were only two keys on the ring, so our chances of getting in there on the first try weren't too bad. Still, I did half-expect us to get it wrong right out of the gate. But, once I heard the lock click, I realized our luck must have finally been changing for the better.

"*It worked!*" Will shouted. He must have been bracing himself for a minor setback as well. The two of us were stuck somewhere between Nervous Nelly and naysayer. I figured it was finally time to ditch those monikers.

Naturally, he was in first. I know I'm not a girl, but it would have been nice if he had held the door for me. Chivalry was clearly dead, but, then again, so were the things that were after us. Well, at one point they were dead. Now, they were something else. And, besides, now that I think of it, who gives a darn about chivalry anyways? I was just glad we were finally safe.

I turned to shut the door behind me, and standing right there with his face pressed up against the window was a zombie. *Holy cow!* I remember thinking. That was close. In all of the excitement, I didn't realize we had one that close behind us. I assumed they were all still sprawled out on the floor, trying to figure out who or what had just hit them from behind – that is if they were even capable of wondering in the first place. But, nope, he wasn't confused at all. He was staring me right in the eyes – or rather right in the 3-D glasses.

I quickly snapped out of it, and went to lock the door from the inside. The only problem being there was no way to do so.

"*Oh, man! Please let this lock automatically,*" I pleaded.

"It does," Will said. "Don't worry."

I didn't even ask him how he could be so sure of it. I just accepted his response and stepped away from the door. A few more of them had gathered at the window. I needed Will to be right now more than ever. If he wasn't, then we were goners.

A few seconds later, we discovered it wasn't just the undead at the door anymore. The living had surprisingly joined them there as well. I realize that's probably a tough one to wrap your head around. What I meant was the store manager - or whoever he was - was now staring at us as well.

What was he thinking? Talk about throwing caution to the wind. I mean, this guy was taking the mother of all chances. I got so nervous I couldn't even watch. I had to cover my eyes.

I heard a knock at the door, but it wasn't enough for me to lower my hands. I also didn't lower them when I heard the doorknob jiggling. *No, thank you.*

"I wonder what *he* wants," Will said. "And, why the heck aren't they attacking him?"

This was finally enough for me to uncover my eyes. This didn't make any sense. I mean, he was right there, leaving himself wide open for them.

"*He must be with them!*" Will announced. "That must be it."

"You think so?" I asked. "That doesn't really make any sense though. Why would they choose to be friends with him, but not us?"

"I don't know, but I'm certainly not gonna open the door to find out. If he's with them, then he's against us."

I nodded in agreement.

Once the guy must have realized we weren't budging, he gave us one last look of disdain and marched himself right over to the register stand. Honestly, I couldn't believe it. They didn't even try to stop him. These things that had been heading us off at every turn let this guy walk right off on his own. That pretty much confirmed Will's suspicions for me. He was definitely with them. And, then, he confused me even further when he picked up the telephone and started flapping his gums about something. He pointed to us a few times to make matters worse. I could only assume he was calling for help, as if *that* was even necessary.

Eventually, he hung the phone up and just stood there, staring at us. Who *was* this guy? And, what did he have against us? To be honest with you, he didn't even look that sinister, but obviously he was. I mean, the proof was in the pudding. Only a sinister guy would have an army of zombies at his disposal, right?

16

THE STORE MANAGER just left us trapped in there for a good ten minutes before moving out from behind the register stand. I say trapped because that was just how it felt. That joker had somehow turned the tables on us. The zombies were still right there pressed up against the window, so we still weren't anywhere near ready to open that door. It just seemed like the guy didn't care whether or not we ever came out. Talk about reverse psychology. I went from feeling safe to feeling trapped. He was *good.*

I figured he was going to join his buddies – or rather his minions – at the door once again, but apparently this wasn't his play. Instead, he made like he was leaving the store altogether.

"Where the heck do you think he's going?" Will asked. "Don't tell me he's going on his lunch break. Talk about an evil dude. And, here I thought dogs smelled evil. They were a lot of help. Not."

I broke into a fit of laughter and struggled to stop. I couldn't tell what had gotten into me. Maybe it was the sheer ridiculousness of it all. Maybe it was my deep appreciation for sarcasm. Maybe it was a combination of the two. I wasn't sure, but, regardless of the reason, I made it seem like Will had said just about the funniest thing in the history of the world.

"I don't know," I answered, still giggling a little. "Um, it looks like he's leaving. Maybe *he's* even afraid of them now. I don't know if that's good for us or bad for us."

"Not sure," Will replied. "But I know I won't be missing him. That's for sure. Zombies are bad enough when they don't have someone telling them what to do."

"Yup," I agreed.

Just when I was getting used to not having him around, he returned – and he wasn't alone. He'd brought a friend. He was the living kind, which I assumed was a good thing. And, actually, he was a mall security guard, which, of course, threw me for a loop. I mean, if I was leading a zombie attack or wreaking any other kind of havoc, then the last person *I'd* want hanging around would be a security guard. Unless, of course, he *wasn't* planning on keeping him around. What if this was a trap and he was planning to sic his zombies on this poor guy? I needed to warn him.

"*Officer! Officer!*" I shouted, waving my arms around like I was on some desert island and he was a ship's lookout.

Before I could warn him, though, the manager quickly pointed us out. The guard shot us a confused look. *Dang it!* Now, he had his back to the guy. Not good. Before I could motion for him to turn around, he grabbed hold of the little CB radio strapped across his shoulder and began speaking into it. *Phew!* He must have been calling for back-up. Crisis averted.

The manager leaned forward to whisper something in the guard's ear, to which he nodded in agreement. For the time being, I felt a little relieved – for the *guard's* safety anyways. However, this did raise a few new questions. For starters, was he there to help us? Secondly, if he wasn't there to help us, then what did he plan to do with us? Finally, and not to sound too repetitive, what did these people have against *us* – two otherwise unimportant ten-year-old kids? None of this made any sense.

"He's in on it, too," I said, with a sigh.

"No way," Will disagreed. "He can't be. He's a security guard. He's supposed to…"

"Protect us?" I interrupted, giving him a worrisome look. "Yeah, he's *supposed* to. There have been quite a few *supposed* to's that haven't exactly gone our way today. Zombies are *supposed* to not exist. Pet store managers are *supposed* to not lead an army of zombies. The ticket booth guy was *supposed* to not let us in to see *Zombies: Too Close for Comfort.*"

"Well, to be fair, he really didn't," Will reminded me. "We snuck in. Remember?"

"That is true," I said. "But you get my point."

"I guess so."

"Anyways, I think he's..." I started to say.

"Headed this way," Will added.

I instinctively looked over at the door to make sure it was still locked, but, alas, there was no way of knowing for sure. I was beginning to hate that door I relied upon so much. He was only about halfway to the door before he glanced back at the manager. He then motioned to the floor – specifically the area surrounding him. From where I stood, I couldn't see exactly what he was pointing out, but I had the feeling it was the pack of dogs gnawing on pig ears at his feet. He flailed his arms around – perhaps trying to get them to vacate the scene, then he shook his head in what I assume was frustration, and, finally, he announced something. Whatever it was, the manager looked kind of upset over it. He even threw his arms up over it. It was like watching a couple of mimes perform and trying to figure out what the heck they were doing.

Before I could take my best stab at it, the manager, too, shook his head and then began waving his customers to the front of the store. As they approached him, he reminded them to grab their dog on the way by. At least, I think he did. Not long after that, he directed them out into the mall. Unbelievable. They cleared the store for us. Nobody looked happy. We even caught some angry looks on the way by. What was their problem? Was it really so important that they got their dog trained? To be honest, all they really needed was a bag of pig ears. Simple as that. They didn't need to pay some dog whisperer for crying out loud. I probably saved them a pile of dough in the long run.

Once the dogs were out of the picture, the guard tried his luck with the door. I felt pretty safe for the time being until I noticed the key ring attached to his belt loop. There had to have been at least a hundred keys on that thing. Was one of them an extra key to *that* particular door? Or, was I giving him a little too much credit? Just to be on the safe side, I urged Will to move over to the window where they kept the puppies – the one that faced the mall. There were always a few people gathered around that window every time I happened by. I figured, if nothing else, at least we'd have witnesses for whatever was about to happen to us. They weren't going to get away with it.

"What do you want to do?" he asked, a little flabbergasted. "Get right in there with them?"

"Yeah," I answered, matter-of-factly. "They probably won't do anything to us with all of those people watching."

He could only shrug his shoulders at this logic.

"It's worth a shot," he said, before stepping up and in.

I joined him. If I'd had a smartphone on me, then I'd have snapped a picture of him in there just because. He would have just stuck his tongue out anyways, so maybe it's a good thing I didn't have one.

The puppies were kind of weird about the whole thing. Who could blame them? I mean, this was supposed to be their time to shine. No humans allowed. Then, all of the sudden, they were invaded by not one, but two humans. Come to think of it, I'd have probably reacted the same way. One of them slept the whole time. He had no idea we were even in there with him. There's always one of them in there snoozing the day away. Not a care in the world. Couldn't be bothered. *Man!* They had the life. On top of that, they didn't have to worry about what was going on right outside of their window. No zombie in his right mind would eat an adorable, little puppy. For once in my life, I was envious of a puppy. What had the world come to? What had I been lowered to?

"Aw," Will began. "Look at him."

I glanced over to find my best friend – my pathetic best friend – cuddling with one of the little suckers. It was as though he'd forgotten all about the not so cuddly big suckers trying to make a quick meal of us.

"I know," I said, kind of falling into the same trap. "But…"

"But what?"

Of course, I was falling for them. You see, Mom wouldn't let me have a dog on account of the fact that she was deathly allergic to them and I wasn't "responsible enough" to have a dog. So, in a roundabout way, it was her fault I was losing this battle. Will's mom, on the other hand, probably would have let me have a dog. After all, she was….*walking right by us at that instant!*

Wow! Talk about perfect timing. She was with one of the other security guards. I couldn't believe it. I knew we could trust her, and I was starting to think that maybe we could trust the security guards after all.

She stopped by our window on her way into the store. Actually, it was more like she froze at our window, I suppose. She weaved her way through the crowd of onlookers gathered there, which was noticeably larger than the typical group camped out there.

"Um, Will, honey," she began. Even through the glass I could definitely hear the nervousness in her voice. "Why are you and John sitting in there like puppies?"

I could see it in her eyes that she was hoping we were just doing this to be funny – like it was some not so funny practical joke gone south.

"Because of the zombies, Mom," he answered, crushing her hopes just like that.

"What zombies, honey?" she asked, and probably wished she didn't have to.

His jaw dropped. So did mine actually. I mean, how could his mom be in on it, too? Not only was she his mom, but she was also the *cool* mom. She was the one we could talk to about anything no matter how serious or silly it was.

"*Seriously, Mom?*" he frantically asked. "*You, too?*"

"Me, too? Honey, what's going on? What's all this nonsense about zombies?"

"Look around, Mom. It's not nonsense."

He shook his head. I shook mine, too, to help convince her. If nothing else, you could call it a sign of solidarity. She looked all over the area – probably to appease us more than anything. I think she was already pretty convinced she wasn't in any danger. Once she turned back to face us, she shrugged her shoulders, with concern in her eyes.

"Dude, what is she doing?" I whispered. I even covered my mouth with my hand – sort of like a football coach would on the sidelines whenever he's calling a play or whatever it is he's doing. Between covering my mouth and wearing the 3-D glasses, I doubt she could see any of my face. "Is she actually in on this? This doesn't make any sense. She's the *cool* mom."

"*I know,*" he quickly agreed, as if trying to end the conversation before it really got going. Then, he covered his mouth as well. "None of this makes any sense. And, I mean, not only is she the cool mom, but, more importantly, she's actually *my* mom, dude. This is crazy."

"Well, what should we do then?" I asked.

I forgot to cover my mouth this time around, and I think it came back to bite me. Actually, it came back to bite both of us. She shot me the tough mom look. Yikes. This was the first time I'd ever caught it from her. My own mom had shown it to me plenty of times – specifically whenever I knew better than to do something foolish, but went ahead and did it anyways.

"You should come right out here this instant, young man," she said, with her finger pointed to the floor. "You, too." She lifted it to point to Will.

"Well, *I* have to go, but you can stay if you want," Will sullenly said.

What? I'd never been so insulted in my entire life, which granted was only ten years by that point – but still.

"We're a team," I reminded him. "Wherever you go, I go. I'm not going to let you do this alone, even if she is your mom."

If I'm not mistaken, she beamed a little when I said that last bit – just a little though. Nothing too crazy. Clearly, she was still a little miffed. I had an inkling she didn't think we were altogether crazy. I think part of her still figured we were messing with everyone.

We finally climbed out of the window area and made for the door. Will tried to take one of the puppies with him, but I made him put it back. I guess he still had that *it's okay to be a shoplifter during a zombie attack* mentality. Speaking of zombies, as if we had much else on our mind, they were still huddled around the door. We just stood there for a moment, questioning the sanity of actually opening that door. At least, I was anyways. I can only assume Will was doing the same. While I mulled it over, his mom appeared out of nowhere and then weaved her way through the group of zombies, just as she had done with the gawkers at the window.

"You know, they might actually leave us alone," he said. "I mean, look. They're leaving my mom alone. If they're cool with her, then I'm sure they'll be cool with me. And, if they're cool with me, then they'll probably be cool with you, too."

I guess I couldn't really dismiss this logic. After all, it made as much sense as anything else. Besides, my hands were pretty much tied by this point.

"Well, there's only one way to find out," I said, just before I opened this door of fate.

His mother pulled him out the instant she had the chance. It was as though she were pulling him *out* of harm's way instead of into it.

"*Ouch!*" he shouted, rubbing his arm where she had grabbed him. Before I could snicker, she did the same to me.

"What's going on here?" she immediately asked. "Why weren't you two at the movie theater? I've been looking all over for you. It's a good thing the manager called security on you while I was reporting you missing. Otherwise, I wouldn't have known you were here."

We looked to one another, unsure of whether or not we should even mention the zombies again. Was it even worth it?

"Clearly, you were in a rush to get out of the theater," she said, trying to remove Will's glasses. They still wouldn't budge. She tried again, and again she came up short. Of course, this wasn't enough to keep her from getting to the bottom of all this. She tried her luck with mine next. As expected, they wouldn't budge either.

"Okay. What's seriously going on here? What did you two do?"

"Us?" Will asked, going on the defensive. "All we did was put on a pair of 3-D glasses."

She looked at him like he was full of it. If he hadn't been wearing the glasses, then she'd have probably known for sure he was telling the truth. She would have seen it in his eyes.

"*He's telling the truth!*" I interjected. "*Honestly!*"

"You're sure?" she asked, giving him one last chance to come clean. "You're sure you didn't just walk off with a souvenir?"

Will tossed his arms up in frustration.

"*Mom! I can't take them off! Can't you see that?*"

He gave his glasses another good tug just to hammer home his point.

A tear trickled down his cheek from beneath the glasses. I pretended like I didn't see it just so he wouldn't feel any worse. What happened to us was horrible enough. There was no need to make him feel any lower. And, to be honest, I thought I felt some of my own tears on their way.

She pulled him in for a lengthy hug.

"Okay, honey," she said. "I'll tell you what, why don't we head on back to the theater? Maybe there's a trick to getting these off that we just don't know about."

I guess it was possible, but I mostly doubted it. I mean, why did everyone else get theirs off so easily?

"It's worth a shot, I guess," said Will.

I didn't take my eyes off of the zombies as we exited the store. I still didn't trust them.

17

LET'S just say the long walk back to the theater was nothing short of eerie. I hated it – every minute of it. In fact, the only one of us who didn't seem to mind it too much was his mom. Honestly, the only times she looked at all uncomfortable were the times Will clutched her arm. These were the times the zombies got a little too close for comfort. I know what you're thinking, and, yes, I too am aware of the irony there.

"Honey, you're starting to freak people out a little," she pointed out. "So, do me a favor and just try to be a little braver the rest of the way. Okay?"

He nodded, but I knew he couldn't make any promises. I still didn't get how she expected us to remain so calm. Then again, maybe she was on to something with this whole act calm bit. Maybe the same could be said for people who all of the sudden find themselves drifting into shark-infested water or people who come across bears out in the forest. Maybe if you act calm – or dead in some instances – they leave you alone. Hopefully, I'll never have the opportunity to see if it works with sharks or bears, but I figured it was worth a shot to try it out on zombies while I had the chance.

"Sorry," he apologized. "I'm just having a rough day."

This time, I couldn't withhold my snicker. I mean, seriously, a *rough day*? A rough day is getting a stain that won't come out on your new, white shirt. A rough day is dropping your lunch tray in front of an entire cafeteria of kids and having them applaud you. What we had going on was a horror movie actually coming to life. On top of that, neither one of us knew when or even *if* this movie was ever going to come to an end.

"I understand, honey," she said. "You know what? You're probably just tired. Once we return these glasses to the theater and bring John home, you can take a nap."

Good luck, I came close to saying.

There was no way *I'd* be able to sleep with all of this going on. I wondered how she could be so calm.

Once we reached the theater, we made our way right over to the ticket booth. You know who was there waiting for us. He was sporting the same mischievous grin he had when he first handed us our glasses. I couldn't help but notice a couple of zombies closing in on him. There was a gnawing part of me that really wanted to see them make a quick snack of him, but I was quickly able to force this idea from my mind.

"Hi," Will's mom said. "I was just here about a half-hour ago asking you about these two. Well, as you can see, I've found them."

"Oh good," he said, though I doubted his sincerity. "And just where were the two little angels?"

Suddenly, I was back to hoping the zombies would intervene.

"You wouldn't believe it if I told you," she answered. "Anyways, the reason we're back is because they've wandered off with a couple pairs of your 3-D glasses. They claim they were unable to take them off for some reason. So, would you mind helping us? I'm not sure if there's a trick to it, because, to be honest, I myself was unable to get them off. I'm hoping you have the touch."

"Hmm," he began. "Can't say I've come across this before, but there's a first time for everything, I guess."

He attempted to pull mine off first, and, as expected, he was making no leeway. I felt them shift back and forth a little, which I'll admit gave me some hope, but that was as far as he got.

"No luck yet," he said. "Say, how was the movie? Did the dog end up saving the day?"

If I'm not mistaken, he had something of a gleam in his eye. I think he was onto us. Will's mom offered us both a confused look.

"Didn't you..." she started to ask.

"Actually," I began, looking to Will for the go ahead. He nodded. "We kind of ended up seeing *Zombies: Too Close for Comfort*, sir."

It actually didn't feel too bad to finally have that off of my chest. And, just like that, I finally had something else off – the glasses. I was so happy I could have hugged him, but I didn't, of course. Instead, I simply thanked him.

"Why, you're welcome," he said, with a grin. "But, I'm kind of confused. I could have sworn I gave you tickets to *Dog On It*."

"You did," Will replied. "But that was just a trick, so we could get the 3-D glasses. I'm really sorry about that."

"We both are," I added.

"Aw, that's okay," he said. "No harm, no foul. I was once young, too. And, besides, I think it's safe to say you two have learned a valuable lesson today. You've learned that a lie tends to stick with you for quite a while. And, sometimes, it can even eat away at you, if you let it."

He winked at Will just before he pulled his glasses off with ease. That wink seemed a little strange to me, but I think Will might have been a little too excited to even notice it.

"*Hey! They're gone!*" Will shouted.

"Who?" I asked, dumbfounded.

"Who do you think?" he replied. "The zombies."

My eyes widened, and I quickly took a look around. *He was right!* They weren't there anymore. Not even the ones I thought were going to take a bite out of our new best friend.

"*You're right!*" I shouted, before lifting Will into the air with a bear hug.

"And *this* is why you boys weren't allowed into that movie," the man explained. "Maybe you'll remember this the next time you want to sneak into a movie."

Believe me. There wasn't going to be a next time.

JOHN CADY

John Cady was born and raised in Massachusetts. When he's not busy teaching the English Language Arts to juvenile offenders, he's writing scary stories. These stories can be found in multiple anthologies, including After The Kool Aid Is Gone, It's All Fun and Games Until Somebody Dies, ABC's of Terror Volume 3, and The Dire Circle.

ABOUT THE EDITOR / PUBLISHER

Dawn Shea is an author and half of the publishing team over at D&T Publishing. She lives with her family in Mississippi. Always an avid horror lover, she has moved forward with her dreams of writing and publishing those things she loves so much.

D&T Previously published material:
    ABC's of Terror
    After the Kool-Aid is Gone

Follow her author page on Amazon for all publications she is featured in.
    Follow D&T Publishing at the following locations:
    Website
    Facebook: Page / Group
    Or email us here: dandtpublishing20@gmail.com

Produced by D&T Publishing LLC

Attack of the 3-D Zombies by John Candy

Edited by Patrick C. Harrison III

Cover by Don Noble

Formatting by J.Z. Foster

Corinth, MS

Made in the USA
Middletown, DE
13 January 2022

58096584R10075